D0396493

DEMCO

SAVINGS AND LOAM

Also by Ralph McInerny

Frigor Mortis
Leave of Absence
The Noonday Devil
Connolly's Life
Romanesque
Spinnaker
Rogerson at Bay
Gate of Heaven
The Priest
A Narrow Time
Jolly Rogerson

THE ANDREW BROOM MYSTERY SERIES

Body and Soil
Cause and Effect

THE FATHER DOWLING MYSTERY SERIES

Abracadaver
The Basket Case
Rest in Pieces
Getting a Way with Murder
The Grass Widow
A Loss of Patients
Thicker Than Water
Second Vespers
Lying Three
Bishop as Pawn
The Seventh Station
Her Death of Cold

SAVINGS AND LOAM

AN ANDREW BROOM MYSTERY

RALPH McINERNY

ATHENEUM

NEW YORK 1990

Atheneum
Macmillan Publishing Company
866 Third Avenue, New York, N.Y. 10022
Collier Macmillan Canada, Inc.

Library of Congress Cataloging-in-Publication Data
McInerny, Ralph M.
  Savings and loam : an Andrew Broom mystery /
by Ralph McInerny.
    p. cm.
  ISBN 0-689-12037-0
  I. Title.
PS3563.A31166S25   1990
813'.54—dc20   89-29079   CIP

10 9 8 7 6 5 4 3 2 1

Printed in the United States of America

SAVINGS AND LOAM

ONE

Gunther moved swiftly in a crouch up the hill that overlooked the house. At the crest he dropped and, cradling the M1 in his arms, slithered through the long grass. As he moved, head upright as a turtle's, his eyes were on the house. Fifty yards from it, still in the high grass, he stopped, rolled on his left side, and pulled the phone from the pouch on the right leg of his dungarees. He had dirtied the dungarees, getting the newness off them, dulling the camouflage greens and browns, but they were honestly dirty now. He pulled up the antenna and dialed the number.

A busy signal!

He thought back to the call he had made a month ago. He had telephoned Doremus, a local realtor, and identified himself as Franklin Meecham, a lawyer representing a client who wanted to invest in local property. Doremus Realty, Inc. turned out to be his widow Martha, and the inquiry clearly brightened her day. Why, there were some very interesting properties on the market right now.

"My client is looking for a historic place."

"Historic," she repeated.

"The Krueger farm."

She was overcome with sadness. The Krueger place ("Not that anyone calls it that anymore") was not available, but she had other—

"Who owns it?"

"Willard Palmer."

"My client is prepared to make an offer Mr. Palmer cannot refuse."

A slight pause. "Can you give me a number where I can reach you?"

"I'll telephone you tomorrow at this same time."

"Where is your office, Mr. Meecham?"

"Baltimore. I'm calling from Indianapolis, however. I am prepared to come to Wyler tomorrow. I'll call you before noon."

The following day, with seemingly infinite regret, she told him Willard Palmer would refuse any offer for his place. He had only been in the house for two years and he had invested a good deal of money to make it exactly what he wanted.

"How much did he pay for it?"

"Eighty thousand dollars."

Gunther couldn't believe it, but the house and 150 acres were in northern Indiana. Clearly not a booming market.

"My client will pay him twice that."

"It's worth much more now, Mr. Meecham, but believe me, it's not a question of money. This is the house Mr. Palmer always dreamed of."

"I see."

"I do have some other possibilities I'd like to show you."

"Thank you, but I'll have to speak to my client first. I'll get back to you."

He sat on the edge of the bed in the Indianapolis hotel room, fifty-six years old, iron gray hair, clear blue eyes in which few emotions ever revealed themselves. He did not look like a man whose deepest desire had just been thwarted by a telephone call. But then he could not accept defeat. Delay, perhaps, but never defeat.

In a month since, he had given the matter long, dispassionate thought. He did not have the time nor the interest to find out whether Palmer was as adamant as Mrs. Doremus said. He knew nothing of Palmer and wanted to know nothing. Best to keep the whole thing impersonal. He was lying here in the field engaged on a mission to remove an obstacle to his plans, remove it surgically, impersonally, finally.

He dialed the number again. The ringing began and Gunther's grip on the field telephone tightened.

"Yes?" The voice was bored, prepared to be annoyed.

"Man, what is that thing in your backyard?"

"What?"

"I said what is that god-awful thing in your backyard. Out there by your bar-b-que?"

"I don't know what—"

Gunther hung up, stuffed the phone back into the

dungaree pocket, and unslung the strap of the M1. When he had it strapped to him in the way he had learned in basic training, he sighted on the back door of the house. He realized he was holding his breath. A face appeared at a back window; it was tempting but he waited. This was a drastic solution and he did not want to try and fail. The curtain settled back into place.

Seconds ballooned into immense stretches of time. The interval between taking in a breath and letting it go seemed more than enough for a life to be lived. The numbers on his digital watch looked frozen.

The back door finally opened, and a head appeared. It was Palmer. He looked around the door, craning his neck, turning toward the limestone fireplace built when outdoor cooking was more than popping charcoal briquettes into a grill. The smokehouse had stood near that fireplace.

Palmer was outside now, looking around with a silly grin on his face. Of course, he would think he was being watched. He would think the caller was a neighbor, but who? The tall, patrician figure with the paisley ascot at his turkey throat paused and looked around. Come out, come out, wherever you are.

The upper H of the sight now held Palmer's torso.

Gunther's gloved finger squeezed the trigger, slowly, deliberately. The gun leapt and he was tugged up by the strap. When it came down again, he kept dropping it to where Palmer lay on the grass. He squeezed off another round, and the body lurched and rolled.

And finally lay still. Then Gunther heard the sound of the rifle, the two shots echoing back from the

4

saucer of hills in which the farm stood. He counted to five, as slowly as he could, but Palmer had not moved. Then he began to loosen the rifle strap. He slipped it over his head. It was tempting just to leave it there, but he shook his head. He would stick to the plan.

He crawled back up over the hill, once more cradling the rifle in the crook of his elbows as he went crabwise through the grass. Once over the hill, he stood and, leaning forward, ran on a straight line toward the stand of trees along the river. He felt that he was running through water. Something had happened to the atmosphere—the world had slowed and with it cosmic time and he would never make it to those goddam trees.

He got there. He pressed his back against an oak and looked up into the network of branches and boughs and leaves in constant movement. It was like looking at his boyhood, being back in Baraboo, before Korea and all the shit. How good it would be to climb up there and hide, spend all afternoon in the central Wisconsin of forty years ago. For a chancy moment he knew what it would be like to step outside his mind, lose control, regain innocence by withdrawal.

An ant up his trouser leg snapped him out of it. He tried to dance the little devil free, shaking the leg of the dungarees, but the ant was on his bare leg, under his suit trousers as well. Gunther pressed it from outside, killing it. Then he ran down to the river.

The train trestle seemed to walk on stilts across the river. The duffel bag was where he had left it.

Gunther slipped out of the dungarees and shoved them in the bag. He stripped down the rifle and put the pieces in the bag, hesitating before including the phone. That was a damned good phone.

His civilian clothes were as much of a uniform as the dungarees: blue blazer, gray slacks, striped tie. He slung the duffel back over his shoulder, scrambled up the gravelly bank to the trestle, and then moved gingerly out across it. He could see the muddy river move languorously below him, visible between the railroad ties that made up the bridge. In the center, without breaking stride, he took the duffel from his shoulder and, in a single motion, hurled it out over the water. He did not wait to hear it hit, but continued moving toward the opposite side.

On this side there was a path leading up to the interstate oasis where he had left his rented car. He got behind the wheel, lit a cigarette, and turned the ignition key. Only when he was accelerating onto the interstate did he let out a triumphant shout.

TWO

Leroy White was lying in the back of the van, too tired to fall asleep, when he saw the Cougar come into the lot. Leroy was betting with himself on whether each vehicle would head for the pumps or pull to the front of the lot so everybody could go into the rest stop and take a pee. But this guy did neither, breaking the rules of the game. He put his car way back in the lot, the last row, though there was plenty of room close in.

On the striped mattress beside him Marilys was dead asleep, on her back, mouth open, her breathing deep and satisfied. Leroy smiled. When he made 'em happy, they stayed happy. Doing it in parking lots like a couple kids. Well, why the hell not? Marilys was a kid. Twenty years younger than Leroy, who had left a wife and three young ones to run off with

Marilys a year and a half ago. Ever since, they had been moving across the country, eating off the land, so to speak. It was amazing how well you could live on the generosity of others.

Leroy crawled to the back of the van and looked out the window to where the dude in the Cougar had parked. If he left the car unlocked, Leroy might go see what contributions the fellow might have to make. The guy got out of the car and Leroy didn't see him punch any lock button before he went around behind. The trunk door went up and a minute later went down again. The man was carrying what looked like a duffel bag when he started toward the oasis. A duffel bag? Naw, not someone dressed like that, not someone driving a big old Cougar.

Leroy stepped over Marilys, opened the driver's door, and got out.

"Where you going?" Marilys had sat upright at the sound of the door and looked at him with frightened, unfocused eyes.

"I'll be right back."

He liked the way she never wanted him out of her sight. What the hell she saw in a fat and bald and gray-bearded forty-six-year-old sonofabitch, he never knew, but he liked it. He never regretted kicking it all over and going off with her. He had hired her at the Dairy Queen, a narrow-faced woman who looked like a girl and was very vague as to where she was from and where she had worked before. Which was fine with Leroy—he didn't plan on paying her Social Security anyway. Pay with cash in an envelope if you could, that was his policy. Which was why the

IRS had called him in twice in the previous three years. His fear that they had their eye on him made taking off with Marilys even more attractive.

The first time he made love to her was in his office. It was awful. She did it as if it were the price of the job, which wasn't true. Afterward he said he had known better sheep.

"You're no prize either."

By rights he should have been mad. Insulting his manhood after being about as sexy as a knothole. But he laughed. The side of her mouth went up in half a smile and then her teeth appeared, small and even like a cob of corn.

"Next time'll be better."

She stuck a finger into his belly and left the office.

The next time was at the Borealis Motor Lodge on the west side of Atcheson. The shower dripped like the Chinese water torture and the sheets were gray, but Marilys was really impressed, as if this were luxury. He hadn't expected the tenderness he felt for her.

Two weeks later she gave notice.

"Where you going?"

She shrugged. "West?"

"Why not east?"

"Maybe I will."

God, what a life. He envied her. He was tied down to the goddam Dairy Queen, busting his butt in season and working part-time for the city off-season, sweeping up the goddam water treatment plant. Dorie and the kids despised him, he wasn't sure why, but he felt it. She passed it on to them, probably.

"You want company, Marilys?"

She looked wary. "Who?"

"Me."

She tipped her head and her straight hair hung like a plumb line to her shoulder. "You're kidding."

He pulled open the desk drawer, took out the cash box, and emptied it on the desk. Three hundred and nineteen dollars. Maybe another fifty in the cash register. It seemed a pitiful sum to have worked so hard for. "That's our stake."

"I have a van."

With Arizona plates. She also had the registration card. Marilys Agamata. Maiden name?

"Maiden name," she repeated, as if she had never heard the phrase. "Now, my memory ain't all that good."

They spent that night in the Borealis, at her request. They drove off at four in the morning, going west. Leroy wondered if Dorie missed him. She had the Dairy Queen. If she and the kids worked it together, they would do all right. It wasn't as though he had left them destitute. After a month or so he didn't think of them much anymore. He hoped it was the same with them.

The Cougar was unlocked. No wonder. There was nothing in it. Then he saw the sticker in the back window. Meridian Rental. Indianapolis. Indiana plates. He had gone around the back of the car to check it when he looked up and saw a soldier hurrying across the lot, head down. It was the duffel bag that made him realize it was the driver of the Cougar.

Leroy stepped back out of the lot and into the

brush behind. A bank led down to the river. His heart was in his mouth. The guy had seen him nosing around the Cougar and would want to know what the hell he was up to. And sure enough he came right past the Cougar, heading for the river.

Only he wasn't headed for Leroy. He seemed to know where he was going, taking a path down toward the river and then cutting along out of sight about thirty yards to a train trestle. You don't see many trestles like that anymore, all wood. God, how many trees went into building something like that?

The guy in the fatigues went across the trestle like a football player, lifting his knees high, steady but fast, a man with something on his mind.

Leroy was so relieved he wasn't going to have to explain to the man what his interest in the Cougar was that he sat there above the river and lit up his pipe and enjoyed the peace. He wished Marilys would join him, but she was probably back asleep. She couldn't sleep well at night, but she could lie down on that mattress in the back of the van at any hour of the day and be asleep in a couple of seconds.

Leroy didn't wonder too much about the guy who had changed into camouflage fatigues and headed out over the train trestle. Until he heard the rifle shots. Very distinctive rifle shots. When he was in the Guard, he had qualified on the M1 and he would bet anything that had been an M1. Two shots. Who the hell would be shooting a World War II–vintage rifle in the Indiana countryside? Had to be the man in the Cougar; but why?

A few minutes after the shots, Leroy saw him on

11

the opposite bank. He was getting out of the fatigues, stuffing them into the duffel bag. Sure enough, he had a rifle too, an M1. He broke it down and put it into the duffel bag with the fatigues. Leroy got well out of sight as the man started back across the trestle.

When he let the duffel bag go, Leroy watched it drop toward the water. It struck softly and almost immediately went under, taken down by the rifle. When the man came up the path toward the parking lot, he passed within ten feet of Leroy. Square jawed, mean-eyed sonofabitch. He headed right for the Cougar and lit a cigarette when he got behind the wheel.

Leroy scratched the number of the plate in the dirt, thought a minute, and scratched some words as well. Meridian Rental.

"Where you been?" Marilys didn't open her eyes, just lay there, knowing it was him.

"There's a river back there."

She made a noncommittal sound.

"Want to go swimming?"

She rolled on her belly and looked at him with a crooked smile.

"Do you mean it?"

"Last one in's a monkey's uncle."

Kids, that's what they acted like, a couple of goddam kids, although Marilys got scared when he swam toward the middle of the river, keeping close to the trestle. No danger so long as he could grab hold of that thing. The first time he went under to test the bottom, he couldn't believe it. He could actually stand on tiptoes and keep the tip of his nose out of water.

He found the bag with his feet before he dove for it. Once he had it, he kept it beneath the surface and moved back toward shore.

"I thought you were going to swim across."

"I did. Halfway out, halfway back."

"Ha."

Then she saw the duffel bag. "What's that?"

"Salvage."

"What's in it?"

He opened the neck of the bag and looked in. He'd been right. It was an M1. He showed Marilys the butt of it.

"A broken gun?"

"I can fix it."

"I don't like guns."

"This is a good gun."

He put the bag by the tree and the two of them swam out into the river together.

THREE

Andrew Broom discovered the body of Willard Palmer after the second call from Maxine Shapiro, Palmer's agent in New York.

"Sorry to bother you, Mr. Broom. I know it's dumb to think you all know what the rest of you are doing out there, but I wonder if you've seen Will. I've been ringing his phone off the hook for two days."

Broom smiled. No point in telling Ms. Shapiro that he had seen Willard hardly at all since the artist had moved back to Wyler and bought, of all places, the old Krueger farm. Palmer was about as rustic as Oscar Wilde. Shapiro would probably have picked up her notion of small towns from the movies, but Willard was returning to memories of his youth.

The second time, Ms. Shapiro was less apologetic.

"You're his lawyer, right?"

"Sort of." Andrew had helped Willard with the paperwork when he bought the farm.

"Look, Mr. Broom, I'm worried. Will was supposed to have some drawings here last week at the latest. He is never late. Never. Should I call the police and ask them to go take a look?"

"Don't do that, I'll check in on him."

"Would you let me know right away? I'm being hounded by the publisher for those drawings."

He might have sent Gerald, he might have asked Susannah to go, but it was a welcome opportunity to get out of the office. Talking with Maxine Shapiro reminded him of what a nice life he had in Wyler. Small-town lawyer, sure, but doing very well and with a lot less wear and tear than practicing in a large city would give. For him that would have been Chicago. The one thing he liked for sure about Chicago was the Bears, and even they were an annual agony; he surely had not wanted to let his life tick away in an office in the Loop where he would spend three-quarters of his time dreaming of being somewhere else.

Wyler was the somewhere else. His hometown. He had invested heavily in Wyler, put up the clinic, led the fight for the downtown mall that had meant at least a standoff with the mall on the east side, acres of blacktop and flat gravel roofed buildings, the whole damned thing identical to hundreds of others across the country.

Susannah looked up when he came out of his office. There were moments when he saw her as she had been before they married. This was one of them and it added zest to the kiss he gave her.

15

"Where you going?"

"To service one of my many mistresses."

"Ha. What was the New York call?"

"A lady worried about Willard Palmer."

"A lady?"

"His agent. She can't reach him."

"And you're going out to check on him?"

"Want to come along?"

"If Gerald were here, I would."

In the elevator he wondered where Gerald was. But it was only one-fifteen. Lunches were not generally prolonged in Wyler, but he could scarcely accuse his nephew of goofing off. After all, he had persuaded him to join him in Wyler because it was a more humane environment. And more varied and interesting from a legal point of view. Where but in Wyler would the most successful lawyer in town run an errand he could have sent a kid on? Or the sheriff.

The Krueger farm was out County Road 16, which had been nothing when Andrew was a kid. But the interstate changed that, and then they put up the Tarkington Oasis five miles out of town, providing employment for a significant number of locals. The road had been widened and even expanded to four lanes for the first mile out of town. Where it went by the Krueger farm, Route 16 looked pretty much as it had in the fifties when the place had been abandoned. The house, that is. The land was rented out, but the large brick house stood empty, its windows staring blankly toward the hills that surrounded the property. The outbuildings were solidly built too, their lower halves brick like the house.

In the late fifties, Harris, the man who was leasing the land, bought the place. He couldn't really afford it. The house had suffered during the years it hadn't been occupied, no doubt, and it would have taken money to get it back to what it had once been. Andrew's father was his source for that, going on about what a picture that farm had been.

What happened to the Kruegers?

His father thought about it, as if the question genuinely puzzled him. "They left," he said finally.

"But why?"

"Damned if I know. The boys went to the war, but the old man was too old for that."

He meant World War II. There was only one war for men his father's age. But then he carried a souvenir of it around with him in his gimpy walk.

The house had an abandoned look when Andrew turned in the drive and slowed the car, crawling up the blacktop road bordered by untrimmed hedges. The windows of the house looked as they had when he was a kid, the half-drawn blinds giving them a lidded look as they stared unblinking at the world. He came to a Y, giving him a choice between going left to the front door or around the house to the garages. He went around the house.

He saw the body before he came to a full stop in front of the garages.

He sat behind the wheel, staring at the ungodly mess, before he pushed open the door and went reluctantly across the lawn to where the remains of Willard Palmer lay. The poor guy had come back to Wyler to die—his very own words when he signed

17

the papers for the house. Whatever had happened had happened a while back, because animals had been at the body. In fact, Andrew's first thought was that Willard had been brought down by a pack of wild dogs.

Willard's limbs were set like those of a swimmer, and the side of his face that was exposed was badly mangled. Andrew crouched, about to turn the body over, but stopped. It wasn't simply caution. His gorge was rising. He went back to his car and phoned Susannah.

"Call Cleary and tell him to get out to the Krueger farm. Willard Palmer is dead."

"How did you get in?"

Andrew had to smile. Leave it to Susannah to react in just that way.

"I found him lying in the backyard."

"I'll put you on hold while I call the sheriff. I want to hear more."

"Is Gerald back?"

"Just this minute."

"Then come out here."

While he waited, Andrew kept clear of the body, walking to the stone fence at the back of the lawn. It was not the kind of fence you saw much around here. Old Krueger had put it up, piece by piece. How had it lasted so long without any cement? As far as Andrew could see, the stones were loose. Beyond the fence was corn, and the nearby stalks were pretty chewed up. Racoons. Would racoons mangle a corpse?

His eyes lifted to the hills that rose gently about a hundred yards back. Off to the right would be the river. Had Willard played there when he was a kid? Andrew had, but his memories might have been of a place thousand of miles away, so far as revisiting them went. The trouble with living at home was that everything was always right there, waiting for you when you decided to take a look at it. So, of course, you never did.

The first thing he said to Susannah when she arrived was that he wanted to take her on a hike along the river.

"I'm not dressed for it."

"I was thinking of the weekend."

"I can't think of anything else."

It was ghoulish to laugh like that, but it was their favorite Marx Brothers joke—Chico playing the piano like crazy and telling Groucho he can't think of the ending and Groucho saying he can't think of anything else. Sheriff Cleary pulled up behind Susannah's car and came toward them with the wary look of one whose leg has been pulled before. Andrew pointed across the lawn.

"Judas Priest," Cleary said, and then, leaning forward as if following his nose, he moved across the lawn toward the body.

Susannah was trying not to look at Willard.

"He's been dead for days," Andrew said.

"Good heavens."

Shot twice was Cleary's guess, and it was borne out when Widmann, the county coroner, arrived. Cleary wanted to remove the body to the morgue immediately, but Widmann dithered, walking around the yard, looking back at the hills. When he started off in that direction, Andrew went with him.

They found the cartridge shells about fifty yards back. From the way the grass was matted down, Cleary guessed that the sniper had lain in wait there.

"Just waiting for Willard to come outside?"

"Maybe he knew his habits."

"He?"

"Whoever."

"You know what I think?"

"Tell me."

"That's a thirty-caliber. I say it was an M1. Know what an M1 is?"

The only M1 Andrew knew was the money supply. He waited and Cleary told him it was the rifle that had won the Second World War. Andrew took the shell casing and turned it over. His father would have shot a few of these.

"So we got a murder," Cleary said.

"Now all you need is a murderer."

FOUR

At the country club Gerald looked wise when he was asked about the murder of Willard Palmer but said nothing, largely because he had nothing to tell. But the assumption was that Gerald knew whatever Andrew Broom knew and, after all, his uncle had discovered the body.

"What was he doing out there anyway?" Foster of the *Wyler Dealer* wanted to know. "He never did get along with Willard."

"He was his lawyer," Gerald said.

"So what was he doing out there? Willard didn't call and ask him out. By then he'd been dead two days."

"Nearly three."

It was the question Gerald had put to his uncle. Maxine Shapiro, Willard's New York agent, was the answer. Well, it was as much of a New York case as anything. All Willard's old enemies in Manhattan were being questioned at Maxine's insistence. She provided a list, supplementing the massive Rolodex Willard had in his studio. Those names were business contacts, but Maxine obviously thought that Willard's death was connected with what she rather demurely called her client's "sexual orientation."

"He went out there to reform," she had told Andrew—with Gerald and Susannah listening in on other phones. "It wasn't just fear of his health, although that was part of it. Willard had what I can only describe as a religious conversion. And maybe some of his old friends didn't like his change of heart."

It wasn't much to go on. Furthermore, the remote investigation of all Willard's old friends was a not very welcome distraction from current business. Andrew had promised Gerald that the practice of law in a town the size of Wyler would be interesting. That was proving to be an understatement. They were due in court at the beginning of the week defending Glen Olson on a manslaughter charge; a Chicano farm laborer had been found dead on Olson's property, pinned beneath an overturned tractor. What would have been considered a tragic but common farm accident turned into something else when the other migrant workers accused Olson of killing Esteban because he had been carrying on with Olson's daughter Gloria.

Gloria Olson was thirty, unmarried, weighed something like 225, and though she had a pretty face, it was not one to launch a thousand ships or to ignite the passions of even the most lovesick migrant worker. Esteban had been twenty, with a wife in Texas, and had worked for Olson three summers running. Andrew was defending Glen Olson.

"Is he innocent?" Gerald asked his uncle.

"That's what he says."

"What do you think?"

"What the Constitution advises. I assume he is innocent."

And until a week ago it had seemed incredible that charges had been brought. In part, the county prosecutor, Grmzchak, was determined that his jurisdiction retain its reputation for evenhanded justice. In part, he was plainly impressed by what the other workers told him. It was common knowledge, they said, that Gloria and Esteban had been having an affair.

"That's a lie," Glen said, after working his jaw. "Why do they blacken the man's name like that? Let him rest in peace."

"I want to talk to Gloria," Andrew said.

"No."

"Why not?"

"I don't want her to even know of these ugly rumors."

"Can't she read?"

"What do you mean?"

"The newspaper has been pretty blunt about it."

"That's Grmzchak's fault."

"Well, it's the chief reason he brought charges. If Gloria was seeing the young man—"

"She was not seeing him nor was he seeing her."

"I want to talk with her, Glen."

Glen Olson acted as if he would rather run the risk of a guilty verdict than subject his darling daughter to any questioning—even from so friendly an inquirer as her father's lawyer. Finally, he brought in the girl—he always referred to her that way—but he insisted on staying in the room while she was questioned. Gerald stayed too.

Gloria, a mountain of pale flesh in a polka-dot dress that was normally reserved for Sunday, tried unsuccessfully to get into one of the armchairs in the conference room. Susannah brought in a plain chair and eased the girl down on it. She looked around the room with bright curious eyes, a little bowed smile on her lips.

"Daddy described this room to me, but it's even nicer than he said."

"Thank you, Gloria. You understand why your daddy has been here, don't you?"

"The girl isn't retarded," Glen said.

"Your father has been accused of arranging the accident that killed Esteban Sanchez."

"I know."

"The other workers say that Esteban was in love with you. Is that true?"

"I don't know." She put a fat little hand over her mouth as if to conceal the smile.

"Did you know Esteban?"

"Yes."

"How well did you know him?"

"He had worked for Daddy before."

"Did you like him?"

"I like all the workers."

"What I meant, Gloria, was did you especially like him."

Glen said, "What he means, Gloria, was were you carrying on with that boy."

She shook her head vigorously, squeezing her eyes shut as she did.

The whole interview would have been useless if Susannah hadn't shown Gloria to the ladies' room when she asked for it. She pulled up the sleeve of the polka-dot dress and showed Susannah the tattooed cross high on her upper arm.

"Esteban?" Susannah asked.

The girl nodded. "Don't tell Daddy."

So there was motive indeed. Glen's performance in the office made it clear enough what he would do if he thought a migrant worker was fooling around with his daughter.

"He did it, Andrew," Gerald said when the three of them were discussing Gloria's ladies'-room revelation.

"Did what?"

"Killed Esteban."

"Esteban was crushed under an overturned tractor."

"He could have arranged that."

"That's what the prosecutor is going to try to show, and I don't envy him his task. A gun or a knife would be different; given a weapon like that, some kind of case can be made. But a tractor? No, I don't think we're in serious trouble at all, even if Gloria's affair is proved in court."

But that was before Grmzchak disclosed the exis-

25

tence of the ramp up which Olson had directed Esteban to drive the tractor. It had been slapped together with two-by-fours and plywood, and two boys and a girl had seen Olson standing on the far side of the ramp, beckoning Esteban forward. The incline was such that three-fourths of the way up the tractor tipped backward and Esteban was crushed beneath it. A grim detail was that he had died slowly, suffering for nearly an hour before Olson even called the hospital. It was another half-hour before help arrived. By then the whole work force surrounded the scene, and frenzied, ineffectual efforts to get the tractor off Esteban were under way. When Cleary (whose Spanish was poor) finally understood about the ramp, he initiated a search, which had at first proved fruitless.

But two days ago the ramp had been found at river's edge, where it had come to rest after having been tumbled down the cliff. Andrew frowned when he heard this but said nothing.

"The wood came from Borden's lumberyard," Gerald continued, reporting what Cleary had told him. "Borden will testify that Olson purchased two-by-fours and plywood."

"Can he identify the particular boards?"

Gerald said nothing. If that was the best retort Andrew could come up with, Glen was doomed.

On Friday, Grmzchak quite unexpectedly asked for and was granted a postponement of trial.

"Circumstantial evidence is always risky," Andrew observed when Grmzchak stopped by. "I don't blame you for holding back."

"I'm indicting him for another crime, Andrew," Grmzchak said.

He looked at Gerald and Susannah before once more facing Andrew. It was a righteous, unrelenting expression, as if Grmzchak felt his office required him to let no misdeed go unpunished.

"Littering the river bank?"

"Finding that ramp by the river is what gave me the idea. Whoever shot Willard Palmer approached the property from more or less that point on the river."

"Is that right?"

"Are you aware of the kind of remarks Glen made about Willard and having 'his kind' living around here?"

"You don't seriously mean to accuse him of shooting Willard Palmer?"

"I'll be arraigning him tomorrow morning."

"You've definitely decided?"

Grmzchak rose. "Yes."

When the three of them were alone in the office, the silence was unbroken for five minutes.

"Grmzchak's a fanatic," Andrew said finally.

"Glen was in the army," Susannah said.

Andrew ran a finger down the line of his nose. "The weapon hasn't been found?"

Gerald said he would check.

"In many ways this will be an easier charge to defend him on," Andrew said. "As soon as the murderer is found, Glen is off the hook."

"Simple," Gerald said.

FIVE

After scratching the license number of the Cougar in the dirt, Leroy copied it onto the inside of a match book and stashed it in the glove compartment. Marilys hadn't shown much curiosity about the whole episode, and Leroy wasn't sure what he meant to do about it. He had had the feeling he'd drawn the big number at Lotto when he pulled up that duffel bag, but he also knew it represented danger. Several days went by before he knew what the danger was.

Marilys wanted to push on. It was their life, pushing on, tumbling tumbleweeds, in the words of the song they loved to sing as they rolled across the highways of the nation, the interstates, the old federal highways, state highways, right on down to county roads. They showed no favorites. In the days after fishing up the duffel bag, Leroy cruised the roads around Wyler, Indiana.

"You seen one of these farms you seen 'em all," Marilys grumbled.

"The breadbasket of the world."

"Corn? Soybeans? What kind of bread you been eating?"

The third day, coming along a road that paralleled the river where the Cougar man had crossed the trestle, Leroy slowed down when he saw the ambulance and the sheriff's cars and lots of other cars beside.

"Don't stop," Marilys said.

"Just taking a look."

"Someone must be sick."

"Sick to death by the look of that traffic jam."

He sure as hell didn't mean to stop; Marilys had no worry on that score. They were no longer folks like these folks and there was no use pretending otherwise. Leroy knew what the kind of people he used to be thought of what he had become with Marilys. So he slid right on past, going maybe twenty miles an hour, not drawing any attention to the two of them.

"You seen enough of this neck of the woods?" Marilys asked that night, lying beside him in the van, the back doors wide open to the starry night. They were parked in the interstate oasis where he had seen the Cougar. The constant roar of the traffic under the restaurant that spanned the four lanes, the growl of the semis as they cranked up the gears getting out of there, the electric hum of the oasis—all these were screened from their hearing, too constant an accompaniment to be audible. Somewhere maybe a hundred yards past his toes was the river and across that and over a hill or two was the farm where they had seen the ambulance and the sheriff cars and all the rest. There had to have been reporters there too. Leroy was looking forward to morning and the local paper.

"You in some rush, honey?"

"How long you suppose we been hanging around this neighborhood?"

"Tomorrow will be the fourth day."

She pressed tightly against him. "It's got something to do with the gun you found in the river, doesn't it?"

"I am a little curious."

"You think someone was killed and that gun was the weapon used. Leroy, it's none of our business."

"Remember the man in the Cougar?"

She rocked her forehead against his rib cage as if to imprint the shaking of her head into his chest. "Forget it, Leroy. We're just tumbleweeds, remember?"

"Wanna tumble?"

Did Marilys want to tumble? The great thing about her was the answer seemed almost always to be yes.

"Now who's the cougar?" she growled in his ear, pinning him to the mattress. "Are you up to a second round?"

"Look and see."

Horny truckers all around them, suburban families pushing through the night, the kids asleep in the back of the station wagon, salesmen wishing all those salesmen jokes were true, and here was Leroy White starring in his own private porno movie in the back of a 1969 VW van. It was almost enough to make him forget that rifle and the Cougar and all those people gathered at that farm that afternoon, which was what Marilys doubtless had in mind. It might have worked too if he hadn't picked up the *Wyler Dealer* when he went in to buy them a couple of cans of Mellow Yellow.

Willard Palmer, age forty-five, had been found shot out in back of the farmhouse he had bought as a haven from Manhattan two years ago. A sniper had fired at least two times from a small hill overlooking the property. Several days had intervened between Palmer's death and the discovery of the body. Andrew Broom, prominent local attorney, had visited his client at the request of Palmer's New York agent and found the corpse. The investigation was proceeding.

"We know who did it," Leroy told Marilys.

"No we don't. You're guessing and I wish you'd stop it. Leroy, promise me we'll get out of here today."

"I figured we'd head for Indianapolis."

She was ecstatic. He was thinking of Meridian Rental. He was also marveling at what a plan the man in the Cougar had come up with. Parking at the oasis, changing into the dungarees, taking the trestle across to the other side of the river, settling down on a hillside, and then picking off Willard Palmer at leisure. No hick sheriff was going to figure that out. Besides, Leroy had the murder weapon.

Except that it wasn't in the well with the spare tire and jack and marijuana where he had put it. He looked up and Marilys, in the passenger seat, turned away.

31

"Where is it?" he asked quietly.

"Back where you found it."

"In the river? Come on. You had no chance to do that."

"Oh yes I did. This morning about four-thirty. I took it out of there and went down to that trestle and pitched the damned thing in. It's bad luck, Leroy. I know it is."

"Show me where you threw it."

"No!"

He came around to the side of the van, put his folded arms on the window and leaned in toward her. "Let's not fight over this, Marilys."

"That's just what I'm saying."

"I want that duffel bag, Marilys. We'll go get the duffel bag and then we're heading south, all right? You want to leave, we'll leave. I want the duffel bag. Let's make it even-steven."

He argued best with Marilys by never raising his voice. She gave up on words fast and cried or shouted or hit at him, losing points like crazy. All he had to do was stay calm and not get mad, and in the end he'd win the fight. He won this one too.

They went hand in hand down the bank to the path and then single file to the trestle. It wasn't twenty feet out in water that hardly covered his knees. He sighted it easily from the trestle and came back to the riverbank, prepared to go down for it, when Marilys called. She was gesturing wildly, and at first he suspected she was still trying to win the argument, but that wasn't like her. He climbed back up the hill to where Marilys awaited him.

There was a man in a sheriff's uniform circling the van. Leroy's first thought was, Thank God Marilys had gotten the duffel bag out of there, but then he thought of the marijuana. The deputy tried the back doors, opened them, and leaned in with his hands on his hips above the leather belt that glistened with bullets and was tugged down by the holster. Leroy hadn't closed the wheel well tightly after discovering the duffel bag was missing. The deputy lifted it, hesitated, and then took out the plastic bag, turned and held it up to the light. Next to Leroy, Marilys took in air.

"What are we going to do?" she whispered.

"Let me think."

There was a pleased, grim look on the deputy's face as he started toward his cruiser.

"I'll get him talking. You look at his tires."

Leroy walked across the blacktop to the van, a big smile of his face, ready to greet the deputy when he noticed him.

"Howdy, officer."

"You belong to this van?"

Leroy smiled and shook his head. "A real collector's item."

"This yours, too?"

Leroy frowned at the plastic bag. "Plastic bag like that could belong to anyone."

"What's in it?"

"You're holding the bag." He couldn't see Marilys anymore. She had gotten behind the cruiser and with any luck it was going to start tipping south pretty soon.

"You got any ID?"

"Officer, I don't mean any disrespect, but why would you ask me for ID? I just stopped to say hello to you and right off you go official on me."

"Is this your van?"

"No."

"You said it was."

"I said it was a collector's item."

It was like arguing with Marilys. The fellow was in his early thirties and must have been much given to fatty foods. He was overweight in an unhealthy-looking way, and it was obvious he enjoyed being a deputy sheriff.

"I want to see your driver's license, mister."

"But I'm not driving."

"Then give me some identification, goddammit."

"Is that your vehicle over there?" Marilys hadn't left a breath of air in either of the tires on the far side and she was now making a wide circuit to get back to the van. The deputy nodded and turned.

"What the hell!"

He ran jangling and jiggling toward the cruiser and Leroy dashed for the front of the van. Marilys hopped in beside him as he turned the ignition key and they moved at a safe but rapid speed out of the lot. In the rearview mirror the deputy, still holding the plastic bag of marijuana, was looking at his two flat tires as if he were going to cry.

SIX

Martha Doremus's first thought when she heard of Willard Palmer's murder was that she was going to be stuck with the Krueger place again. Andrew Broom had insisted on such complicated terms that Willard had the option of bowing out without penalty to himself for two full years after what should have been the closing.

"You act as if he isn't coming home for good," she had complained to Andrew.

"If you're asking whether I think it's a good thing Willard is coming back to Wyler, the answer is emphatically no."

"Well, the farm is a good investment, short- or long-term."

"Is that why it's been on the market for so long?"

"People are so darned superstitious."

"Superstitious?"

"It has the reputation of being bad luck. For goodness sake, don't tell Willard that."

"You're brightening my day."

"It's all a bunch of nonsense. The place was empty for nearly ten years at one time and that made people think of it as haunted or something. But Willard can move in there and live happily ever after."

Finally, almost despite Andrew Broom, the deal (such as it was) went through. Willard had been delighted with his rural retreat; he told Martha he worked well in his native surroundings and wished he'd thought of coming home long ago.

What was the word she thought of when she talked to him in person? Decadent? But then why decades of the rosary? Willard had looked as if he'd been burning the candle at both ends, but after a couple months in his new house the color returned to his cheeks and he looked rested and wholesome. He still dressed in an odd way, little neck scarves, and dyed his hair, trying to look half his age. Honestly, he was more like a woman than a woman was.

Maybe the sale hadn't been nailed down in the usual way, but Martha had grown comfortable with what Andrew had drawn up. Willard was in effect buying an option to buy in two years and if he did, the option money would go toward the down payment. Meanwhile, he had invested the money he had set aside for the house and was going to get an even better bargain eventually than if he had bought it outright. Martha just considered the house sold and that was that—until a month ago when she had gotten that strange call from the Baltimore lawyer inquiring about the Krueger farm.

When it rains, it pours? Maybe. But the call had made her nervous and she had stretched the truth, pretending to have talked with Willard about entertaining an offer he couldn't refuse. The last thing Martha wanted was to have that sale an open question again. Her late husband had tried unsuccessfully for years to sell the place, but the best he had been able to do was to rent the land, and from time to time the house as well. But no one had been interested in buying the place. Now that Martha had Willard in there (and happy too) she had no intention of opening it all up again. So she lied and told the lawyer—Franklin Meecham, she had written it down—that the present owner wouldn't sell for all the tea in China. She had been all set to suggest other possibilities, one of them a good deal more attractive than the Krueger place, as far as Martha was concerned—but the lawyer just cut her off, hanging up.

She had been relieved. She remembered when Willard had called her from New York telling her of his plan to settle down where he had been born and raised and would she find him a suitable retreat, something comfortable, isolated, a pleasant view?

"You could be describing the Krueger place," Martha had said, testing the waters.

"Really? Where is it? In town?"

"You want seclusion. No, it's a farm."

"A farm! My dear lady, I have no intention of

37

becoming a horny-handed son of toil, no matter what my enemies say. A farm! No thank you."

"You don't have to farm. It's like a hundred and fifty acres of lawn," she lied. "It sits in a saucer of hills. It is isolated, yet close to town."

"Where did you say it was."

"Out County Road 16."

"I'd be lying if I said it rang a bell. Could you send me a picture of it?"

She spent the afternoon taking Polaroids, and she sent him a little album of irresistible shots of the house, inside, outside. When he came out to see it, the highest praise he had was that it was exactly like the pictures she had sent him. He wanted it. He wanted to know how quickly he could have it. If she had had the brains of a bird, she would have typed up an offer of purchase then and there and forestalled the roundabout method Andrew Broom came up with. But she was being blasé and nonpushy lest his suspicions be aroused. Later she had been sure Andrew Broom would bring up all the ridiculous talk about the Krueger place being somehow tainted, but to her surprise he didn't know anything about it.

And now Willard was dead, found by Andrew Broom of all people. Why did Willard's violent death seem to bring it all to a natural close? He had defied local superstition and bought an unlucky place—and had paid for it with his life.

Martha would no more have said that aloud than she would have denied the Nicene Creed in the town square. She felt silly enough just thinking it. But in the dark, unbaptized depths of her soul, she believed it.

"What on earth happened out there?" she asked Susannah.

"It's all in the paper. And more."

"Who would want to shoot a man like Willard?"

"Andrew would call that a leading question."

"Just because he was a bit of a sissy?"

"I think it was a little more than that."

"Okay, then it was. But he was leaving all that back in New York."

"Maybe it followed him here."

"Oh, dear."

"Well, it can't have been an accident, Martha. Maybe one shot could have been a stray, some nitwit shooting a high-powered rifle and not paying attention to the distance it travels. But not two. And there's pretty good evidence the assassin was lying in wait on the hillside behind the house."

One thing Martha gave Susannah credit for, she told a person what she knew without a lot of cat and mouse. Andrew Broom would have clammed up and looked wise and that would have been the end of it. Andrew was lucky to have found a woman like Susannah after the tragedy of his first wife—but then most people thought Susannah was lucky too. Martha loved Susannah's hair and the clear eyes that always looked right into yours when she talked. You never had the impression that Susannah was anxious to get on to something more important than having a conversation with you.

"Do you think it was one of his old enemies from New York?"

"Or one of his old friends."

For all Martha knew, the man who had called and identified himself as a Baltimore lawyer named Franklin Meecham could have been one of those New York people. It would have been only fair to mention that call to Susannah, but Martha didn't. There was something she wanted to do before she mentioned that call to anyone.

Back in the office she got directory assistance for Baltimore and asked for the number of Franklin Meecham, an attorney. The voice with its distinctive accent became a hum as the seconds passed and then: "Would you spell that again?"

"I may have it wrong. Meecham. Maybe it's only one *e*."

There was no Meecham, Mecham, or Meacham among the lawyers practicing in Baltimore. There was a Franklin. Martha took the number and called; but after several minutes of being grilled about who exactly she was and what the purpose of this odd call was, she was certain that Franklin was not the man who had called her. Martha managed to bring the conversation to an embarrassing close.

That decided her against mentioning the Franklin Meecham call about the Krueger place.

She was reenforced in her decision when Grmzchak brought charges of murdering Willard Palmer against Glen Olson.

Right away it clicked. She could believe Glen would feel very strongly against having a man like Willard Palmer living in Wyler or its environs. Once Glen had allowed members of a group calling themselves the "Indiana Minutemen, Second to None" to use his farm for what the *Wyler Dealer* had described as "military maneuvers." Glen objected in a lengthy op-ed piece, describing the Indiana Minutemen, Second to None as a patriotic organization, modeled on the militia of Revolutionary America. He also suggested that if the newspaper wanted a quarrel, they should pick it with the citizens of the thirteen original colonies.

The accidental death of Esteban Sanchez on Glen's farm was going to have to wait the prosecution of these new charges. Martha was dumbfounded to learn that Andrew Broom would defend Glen in this second indictment as well. Honestly, you could almost think Andrew had been in cahoots with Glen.

Martha Doremus resolved to have lunch with Susannah real soon and find out what on earth was going on.

SEVEN

Gunther had headed toward Chicago when he drove out of the Wyler Oasis in the rented Cougar. He turned in the car there and took Amtrak to Minneapolis, buying the ticket under the name of Franklin Meecham. He did it on an antic impulse, but as the train swayed through Wisconsin, it seemed in retrospect to have been an inspiration. If his fictive persona performed real deeds in the real world, it would serve his purposes better. And his purposes were to be linked in no way whatsoever with what had happened in Wyler, Indiana.

When the train went through the Dells district, it was all Gunther could do to stay aboard. God, how wonderful it would be to rent a car and just drive around, visiting Baraboo, Lake Delton, Wisconsin Dells, Portage. When he was a kid, there had been signs along the highway, HAVE A SWIG WITH NIG, advertising a bar in Lake Delton. World War II amphibious vehicles had been put to work in the tourist campaign. Baraboo was the town where the Ringling Brothers Circus had originated. Surrounded by these towns, Gunther sometimes thought of his childhood as right out of Walt Disney. The all-American boy.

His face hardened at the thought. He remembered the prewar *Vereins* and Bunds, which had featured speakers like Charles Lindbergh, another all-American boy. And his grandfather had told him of the far worse situation during World War I. German-Americans had changed their names to Anglo-Saxon versions, seeking anonymity, repudiating their heritage as if it were something shameful. His grandfather had told Gunther stories from *his* father about the Irish attack on German Catholics. Once the family had been Catholic, but no more, not after Archbishop Ireland.

This bitter family lore had been the beginning of Gunther's avocation, the study of German-American immigration. He had spent several nights in Leo House on Twenty-third Street in New York, a *Verein* set up to smooth the entry of Catholics from Germany into the new country. There wasn't anything left of that function now, but it was the history of the house that interested Gunther.

After service in Korea, Gunther had spent a second hitch in Germany. Think of it, allied armies still occupying Germany nearly half a century after the war. Only by seeing that the Germans were making a good thing of it, sparing themselves the real costs of defense, could he find it tolerable. Half the occupation force was black besides, an ironic punishment for Nazi racism. That German tour had been the germ of the idea for the import business that had made Gunther's fortune, bringing in German microscopes and other precision instruments connected with science and medicine. He had a Volkswagen dealership in Paterson, also; it was too grim a joke to resist, selling to Americans Hitler's dream car of the thirties. Realizing he had more money than he could ever spend, without heirs, a forty-year-old orphan who thought of nothing but his roots, he had begun to collect memorabilia of German-American immigration. In Allentown, at an estate sale, he had found the diary of Gerhardt Krueger at an auction, a record kept in beautiful Gothic script, a pure German style. He paid a dollar for it, a clothbound oblong ledger filled with writing the heirs could not read. He might have urged them to be more concerned with their family origins, but the man who was selling the stuff was named Ryan!

For a year the Gerhardt Krueger ledger had been simply a thing, a memento of a past that was no more. It might have been eyeglasses or silverware. But when he did sit down to read it one night, not really expecting to get caught up in it, he did not go to bed until three, and he was up again at six, reading the Gothic script by the first light of dawn. At the estate sale he had read a page dealing with slaughtering pigs and had assumed the ledger was full of the details of the Indiana farm that had been Gerhardt's pride. He had a fine descriptive style. The image of the smokehouse formed easily in Gunther's mind as he read, and he could see the Krueger kids scrambling around at the behest of mother and father, the whole family involved in saving food for the winter.

That was an untypical page. Gerhardt, it turned out, was a kind of philosopher. On winter nights it occurred to him to wonder what he, son of a Prussian father and a Silesian mother, was doing there in the middle of Indiana, raising a family that spoke a language he himself did not know all that well. But German culture had come to America and he read a German paper, he taught his children the catechism in German, and on Sunday he was harangued from the pulpit in German.

Yet he was fiercely loyal to this new land. It was part of the American ideal to make a new culture by blending and retaining old ones. The English and the Irish had an advantage as far as language went, but the Irish had no culture and English culture had been present from colonial times. Gerhardt exhibited a surprising knowledge of the Southwest and California, seeing the conquistadors and the California Russians as part of the mixture that was America.

The contrast between the opening thirty or forty pages and the rest was total. Old Krueger had been a young man when the war against the Hun and the kaiser disturbed his sense of belonging in this new land. The sore opened by the anti-German propaganda of the First War never healed and with the rise of Hitler began to fester.

The ledger indicated that Krueger was of two minds about the new Germany. On the one hand, he was stirred by the spectacle of his country rising again from the shambles of defeat and a socialist government. On the other hand, he had the premonition that a new anti-German wave was about to roll across the land. In his ambivalence Krueger began to invest in German industry. Gunther figured rapidly to get a sense of the amounts Krueger was talking about, and he was surprised. His German industry had turned an Indiana farm and prudent purchases of stocks and bonds into a fortune. And, increasingly, that fortune was transferred to Farben and Krupp.

The record of these stock and bond purchases was counterpointed by Krueger's awareness of the fear Hitler inspired. Krueger shared it. He despised this Austrian noncommissioned officer who had the effrontery to speak for Germany. Krueger became increasingly aware of the anti-German animosity in Indiana. Perhaps no one who had not grown up as he had, retaining his German roots, even developing his own private theory of what it meant to be German-American, would have been as sensitive as Krueger became. Sensitive? Call it paranoid. In 1942 he sold the farm and the ledger came to an end.

But not without a startling revelation. Gunther read it over carefully several times; he translated the passage into English. There was no doubt about it. Gerhardt Krueger, saying goodbye to it all, was leaving his farm, his German identity, and an enormous amount of German stocks and bonds, buried behind the house in a spot that could be calculated from the chimney of the house, the smokehouse, and a linden tree.

The burial of those certificates was conducted with typical Krueger care. That he did not simply destroy them was consistent with his lifelong ambivalence. What had happened to the family after that, Gunther had been unable to find out, nor was there any explanation of how the ledger had ended up in an estate sale in Allentown.

★

In Minneapolis, Gunther tried in vain to find the *Wyler Dealer* on sale. There were no wire-service reports of any mysterious shootings in central Indiana. A week after the event, he found a small item in the *Indianapolis Star*, which was subscribed to by the St. Paul Public Library. It was almost as if he needed that enigmatic brief account to know that he had actually done what he had set out to do after the real-estate agent told him Willard Palmer would never let the place go.

Gunther had thought up ways he might conduct a search for the buried stock certificates without harming Palmer, but every idea contained too many possibilities of going wrong. In the end, the most drastic solution also seemed the simplest. Get rid of Palmer and then conduct a search at leisure with no one in the house.

He would have bought the place to establish ownership over the certificates but that way had been closed off by the real-estate agent. Martha Doremus.

That had been a mistake, he thought now. It bothered him to think of Martha Doremus. What kind of woman was she? Would she put together his phone calls and the murder of the occupant of the Krueger house?

It was an unsettling possibility.

EIGHT

No matter what the Constitution says, the task before Andrew Broom was one of proving Glen Olson innocent. The very fact of the indictment, crazy though it was, altered Glen's status irrevocably; add this to his previous indictment in the case of the death of Esteban Sanchez, and there were few citizens who would see the accused as innocent until proof was forthcoming.

"It's all circumstantial, isn't it?" Susannah asked one night. It was after dinner and they were enjoying the September twilight by the pool.

"At best."

"So how can Grmzchak win?"

"By my screwing up."

"Ha. Never."

Good girl. He needed that vote of confidence. He

wondered if she really felt it, and decided she did. In Susannah's eyes he was invincible, but that was because she had never seen him lose an important case. Neither had Gerald, but he hadn't seen that many victories either. Andrew could see doubt creep into his nephew's eyes. Well, Gerald would have been a fool if he thought it was going to be easy for his uncle to get Glen Olson through this unscathed. It had been bad enough trying to get an interview with Gloria. Now it was worse because Glen was perfectly willing to chatter about his dramatic views on the current condition of the country.

"The USA is going to hell in a handbasket," Glen said to Andrew, in a voice that knew no doubt.

"People have been saying that for two hundred years."

Glen waved this away. "It started with Vietnam. All those traitors flying over to kiss the enemy's guns. They should have been shot. Then they rewrote *my* war. Did you ever watch 'M*A*S*H'?"

"Pretty bad?"

"That goddam series, which will probably be reshown as long as 'I Love Lucy,' makes Korea sound like a conspiracy by American generals to assign a few American doctors to the war zone. Any mention of the Commies? Sure. They're all nice guys, of course. Too bad we don't understand them. It's always our fault."

"You watch 'Hogan's Heroes'?"

"That's funny." He said it without smiling.

Andrew wasn't smiling either. He avoided Gerald's

eyes. He wanted his nephew sitting in on all interviews with the client just in case.

"In case of what?"

"In case I see that my perfect batting record is in jeopardy."

"Then I better keep up on it."

"Thanks."

"I'm not thinking of you. I'm thinking of him. Clarence Darrow couldn't get him off."

"He wouldn't have taken Clarence Darrow as his lawyer, not after the Scopes trial."

Clearly, Glen couldn't be put on the stand. Once Grmzchak got him going, he would hang himself. If there was anything surprising, it was that Glen wasn't surprised when he was indicted for shooting Willard Palmer.

"Don't tell me you did it."

"Do you want to know what's behind this?"

"Tell me."

"I backed Rabow against Grmzchak two elections ago. I contributed the maximum to his campaign. Rabow would have been a good prosecutor."

After losing the election, Rabow retired to Arizona. He had been in his late seventies when he ran against Grmzchak. Andrew suggested backing Rabow had been a lost cause.

"Reagan made it."

"You may have a point."

"He'll never forget."

He meant Grmzchak.

What did Grmzchak have against Glen? Only that

Glen was a weapons collector. He called them war mementos. While the howitzer on the lawn in front of his farmhouse was crusty with coats of rustproof paint and would never fire again, in one of the out-buildings he did have an arsenal of still functional weapons, including another howitzer that he shot off twenty times every Fourth of July, obtaining the sheriff's permission in advance.

"Don't think I haven't known Grmzchak was just looking for his chance. I wasn't going to give him one, so he invented an excuse. Two of them," he added after a pause.

"How many M1's you got?"

"I bought a case of them once. Same with car-bines. I've got a Browning automatic rifle too, as good as new. Just don't forget and put your hand on the barrel after you've let go a few rounds."

"How about uniforms?"

"I reached the rank of master sergeant. I still have my dress uniform."

"Field uniforms?"

"You mean fatigues."

"Yes."

Glen shook his head.

"Why not?"

"Ever notice who the best customers of army-navy stores are? Hippies. They've brought disgrace on fatigues."

"That means you don't own any?"

"That's right. I don't."

"But you have?"

Glen thought about it. "I brought some home, sure. I thought they would be practical, but once I got home I could see how funny it was, going around looking like a soldier. That was past."

"So you got rid of them."

"That's right."

Gerald said, "If it was all past, why the weapons?"

"Historical interest."

The Indiana Bureau of Investigation had been all over the hillside behind the Krueger house where the sniper had lain in wait. They had taken casts of knee and elbow prints, and said that the killer had been wearing what appeared to be army fatigues. The guess seemed borne out by the button found on the scene; it was the single physical object they had come up with. The button was army. New.

"So he might have bought the outfit just for the occasion?"

Hanson, the IBI agent, gave half a nod. Maybe he was thinking of the zillion army-navy stores in the country.

"How about the shoes?"

"We got good prints. Want to see them?"

"Army shoes?"

"No. Crepe-soled street shoes. Brand name Rockport."

"Hmmm."

If Hanson had any thoughts about that, he kept them to himself. "He may have worn the fatigues over regular clothes. There was a faint impression of trousers emerging from the legs of the dungarees."

"You're sure?"

Hanson shrugged. "Unless he had the fatigues tailored and pressed. The point of the pantleg's crease is pretty clear in the impressions we took."

"That's all?"

"He had a field phone in a lower pouch on the right leg."

"You can tell that?"

"And that he took it out. He rolled to one side and then settled in to the left of where he had been lying. The phone no longer was there."

"I'm going to put you guys on the Shroud of Turin."

"What's that?"

"A long story."

When they went out to the car, Andrew turned to Gerald.

"I think the guy got Willard out of the house by telephoning him from the hillside."

"Okay."

"Think about it. He buys new fatigues, he pulls them over his civilian clothes and, wearing his street shoes, settles in. Then he phones Willard and gets him to come outside. When he comes out, bang, bang, he's dead."

"We already knew that."

"But now it's vivid."

"Can you see his face?"

"It's not Glen."

"What tells you that?"

"That he didn't buy any fatigues in any army-navy store within easy driving distance of Wyler."

54

"How do you know that?"

"I won't until you check it out."

Andrew himself drove out to the Krueger farm, changed into his jogging costume in the house, left his clothes in the backseat of the car and then, taking his line from where the body had fallen, walked out to the point on the hillside where the sniper had lain in wait. A dozen lathes still stood crookedly, marking the sight, but the string hung with pennants had fallen to the ground, to be found by some archeologist eons from now. He would build on it a theory of the religious practices of the indigenous population.

Andrew Broom rid himself of the thought. After what Hanson had told him, he was prepared to change his judgment of theories elevated on skimpy evidence. He sat above the marked site and looked back toward the house, imagining the killer lying here, waiting, his eyes on the house. He could have spent days waiting if he hadn't thought of a field phone. Nothing easier. Call up Willard and tell him to come outside.

Why would Willard obey? It depended on how the request had been made. When he stood, Andrew looked back up the hill. Presumably, that is where the man had come from. (Hanson's impressions had settled the question of gender too.) Andrew walked up the hill; when he reached the top, he recalled Hanson saying that there were dozens of ways the man could have come to the hillside. He could have come from the east or the west along the hill. He

55

could have come along the river and then climbed the hill. He could have come on the river for that matter.

"Any sign of a boat being pulled ashore?"

"Nothing I'd go to the wall for." Hanson's manner gave no clue as to whether he favored the approach on the river. That opened up two possibilities, of course. The man could have come down- or upriver.

When Andrew got to the river by taking the most direct route from the top of the hill, he looked in both directions. The view upriver was obscured by the train trestle. Andrew had played on that trestle when he was a kid. He smiled, but almost immediately his smile faded. He picked his way along the shore, then scrambled up the gravelly incline and stood looking at the single set of rails; they seemed to meet somewhere beyond the opposite bank. He started across.

When he was a kid, he had gone across the trestle without a thought, moving fast and surefooted over the thing. At forty-five Andrew knew too much to be so foolhardy, and he moved his feet carefully from tie to tie, staring down at the river below. Up to a point, he could see the bottom clearly, but then it went out of sight. On the other side he stood looking back the way he had come. A minute passed before he became aware of a muted steady roar. What was that? He decided to find out. He was halfway up the bank when he thought of the interstate. At the top he found himself looking at the vast expanse of the Wyler Oasis.

He stood on the curbing of the parking lot for twenty minutes, waiting for an epiphany. The trestle and oasis opened up another possible way the killer could have come, he was sure of that.

On the way back, having started across the trestle, he stopped, staring down at the water. It was shallow and transparent and there was something directly below him, seemingly placed at the base of one of the piles on which the trestle stood.

He waded into the water, leaned over, and retrieved the duffel bag.

NINE

Marilys lay sullen and silent, her face swollen more from tears than from his blow while Leroy drove aimlessly on county roads. He could have used some moral support from Marilys at the moment but didn't expect any. At least he could concede to her that she had gotten rid of the duffel bag because she was worried about him. About herself, but about him, as well. He'd tell her as much if she'd cut out the goddam sniffling and get up front where she belonged.

"We gotta get rid of the van, Marilys."

Silence from the back.

"That deputy won't sleep until he tracks us down after what you did to his tires."

"I'm always getting us in trouble, ain't I?"

"No sense getting smartass, Marilys. We need another car."

"Why then let's just buy one."

If she were in her own seat, he would have hit her another one then. What a baby she was. All right if she didn't want to talk. Getting rid of the van and finding other transportation was only half his problem. The thought of that duffel bag pestered him more. How the hell could he retrieve it? He told himself there was less urgency about that. Who was going to find it under water? But would it just stay where she had dropped it? The river wasn't all that active, but it did have a current, maybe currents. Over time, everything in a river moved.

Going back to the oasis was out. The deputy would have called in about the van, every sheriff in the county would be looking for it, all the state cops. Leroy felt that his life with Marilys, which for so long had been one extended and irresponsible dream, was coming to an end.

"Stop the damned whimpering and give me a hand."

"You want me to drive?"

"I'm trying to think."

"Well, I can't help you there, remember? I'm just a dumb bitch."

It was then that Leroy realized why the road he was on seemed familiar. They had been down this one before, the day the body of that guy Palmer was found. The guy who'd been shot by the man in the Cougar. The way to get to the duffel bag was obvious now. Leroy picked up speed and began to hum.

"I'm glad somebody's happy."

"Let's make up, sweetheart, I just figured out how to undo what you did."

"Oh no!"

"Oh yes. We are going to get to that trestle from this side and you are going to show me where you threw that bag."

She crawled up behind his seat. "Please forget that bag, Leroy. Please. We should be getting far away and laying up until they stop looking for this bus."

"We'll do that. Real soon. Just as soon as we fetch that duffel bag."

She groaned, but it was a groan of defeat. Leroy dropped it. No point rubbing it in. She would come along and show him.

"You think you can recognize that place, Marilys. Where they found that body?"

"You just can't wait for trouble, can you, Leroy?"

"It's a big brick house . . . There it is!"

But the triumphant cry died in mid-shout. There was a car parked in the driveway. Leroy was down to twenty miles an hour, resigned to going by, when he figured the hell with it, swung the wheel hard, and damned near tipped the van over as he turned into the driveway.

"Someone's here, Leroy."

"I see that. Someone I can ask for directions."

It was no official car, he was sure of that. A maroon BMW. He pulled the van in behind it and stopped, but he left the motor running. He got out and, as he passed the car, saw the clothes in the backseat. He stopped and looked toward the house. The door of the car was unlocked when he tried it. He went on to the house, looking out toward the back as he did, and pressed the doorbell. Then he began knocking on the frame of the door.

"Jesus, Leroy, cut it out and get back here." Marilys was hanging out the window of the van. "What're you doing?"

He banged on the door some more but something told him no one was going to answer. He ran back to the BMW and pulled open the door. Anyone dumb enough to leave a car like that unlocked might leave the keys. But they were not there. He looked at the pile of clothes.

The keys were in the right trouser pocket. Leroy pulled his head out of the car and looked at Marilys.

"Back up, Marilys, we're leaving."

"You're taking that?"

For answer he slid behind the wheel and put the key in the ignition. When he turned it, the powerful motor came almost silently to life. What a car. They could get a long way in this before they traded it in. Marilys backed up and he followed her, finally making a U-turn that took him out over the front lawn. He was now ahead of her and he turned to go back the way they'd come. It was hard not to gun the BMW, but Marilys in the van was keeping it down, which was probably smart. He bet she was doing it to bug him as well. The thought came that he should floor it anyway and speed right out of the life they had been leading. Maybe it was being in a real car again, but for the first time in a very long time he could imagine acting his age and living the way other people did. What was a man for whom fifty was no longer an unimaginable age doing scavenging across the country with someone like Marilys. She was illiterate, not too smart . . .

She was also a helluva lot more fun than anyone he had ever known before. And their life was about to change pretty radically. Getting rid of the van was going to be hard, but it had to go. It was a ticket to too much trouble.

The road ran more or less parallel to the river, and he kept on it until a crossroad provided the opportunity to go directly toward the river. This was another county road, but a lesser one than Route 16. Not even a number, just the name. Bittersweet Road. It seemed a sign. He was sure Marilys would think so. That was another thing she was, superstitious.

When he knew what he intended to do with the van, he pulled over and stopped. Marilys came up behind and he went back.

"You drive the car. I'm going to drive the van off the road and then we'll give it a push."

"Into the river?"

"I doubt it'll make it all the way down. We'll pick a place where it won't attract attention."

"Maybe we could come back for it some day."

"Maybe."

Not very damned likely, but if she wanted to think so, it was all right with him. No point in scouring the van for clues to Marilys. The vehicles was registered in her name in Arizona. The plates were California plates. They changed them often from the collection they had gathered from interstate stops.

He hadn't seen the ditch, though, and the van got

hung up before he got it properly off the road. He thought of getting the BMW behind it and giving it a push, but there wasn't any point in that. This might be nowhere to them, but people lived here and that van was not going to go unnoticed for long no matter what they did. And he didn't want to risk the BMW.

"We'll just leave it there."

"Right out in the open?"

"Marilys, I think you and I better hit the road. We're going to have to get rid of the car soon too."

"It's all on account of that damned duffel bag," she wailed.

"You're right about that, girl. Get in."

After he got going, he knew it was going to be hard getting rid of the BMW. Marilys ran her hand over the dash as if she expected it to purr, but she was the one doing the purring.

"Ain't this some car, Leroy?"

She punched the radio and stereo music from the tape player filled the car. Western music, but Marilys crossed her bony arms over her big tits and slid down in the seat, ready to enjoy this luxury.

"Check his clothes."

That appealed to her curiosity. She scuttled over her seat into the back. "There's a wallet, Leroy."

"Check it."

"His name is Andrew Broom."

Aha. The man who had found the body. The man who was representing the poor farmer accused of killing Willard Palmer. Some guy named Olson. From his picture in the paper Leroy knew they had the wrong man.

"Leroy," Marilys said in hushed tones. "We're rich."

"How much money in there?"

She was counting half-aloud. There was $473 in the wallet.

"All kinds of credit cards too." She was still waiting for his reaction.

"Get back up here, sweetheart. We're on our way to Indianapolis."

"Let's stay in a motel!"

He smiled at her and nodded. They would stay in a motel. They would dump the car, rent another from Meridian Rental, and maybe spend a couple of days on a little honeymoon.

TEN

Gerald took the call when Andrew telephoned from the Krueger farm to announce that he had found a duffel bag that could very well contain the murder weapon.

"It also contains the fatigues and the field telephone."

"Glen Olson didn't buy anything from the army-navy store in town."

"Forget that. What I have here is hard evidence. We can have tests made to see if this is the gun that was used to shoot Willard. There should be prints."

"And you're sure this will clear Glen?"

A pause. "Either it will or I'm a monkey's uncle."

"I resent that."

"Another thing. My car's been stolen."

"What?"

"My wallet with all my identification, credit cards, and cash is missing. And my clothes."

"You're naked?"

"I changed into my jogging clothes before checking out the river. Like an idiot, I left everything in the car. Anyway, it's missing. Call the state police."

"And the sheriff."

Andrew laughed. "If you like."

"We're talking about the maroon BMW?"

"Which argues that the thief has taste. Susannah will know the license number. Let me talk with her."

"She's not here."

"Then look up the number of Hanson of the IBI, would you? I'll get in touch with him while I'm waiting to be rescued."

"You want me to come get you?"

"I'd prefer Susannah."

"I don't blame you. Are you sure you're dressed?" The words were out before he could stop them. It was not the sort of remark Gerald made to his uncle. Andrew felt free to advise Gerald on his social life, arguing that you had to be in Wyler a long time before you learned to read all the signals right. What he meant was he didn't want Gerald going out with Julie McGough, the daughter of his old enemy and rival, Frank McGough.

"Where do you suppose Susannah is?"

"She can't be far. She didn't leave a note."

"If she returns before you leave, have her come."

Gerald found Hanson's number and, after he had hung up, called the state police. He was put on hold and took the canned music for half a minute before hanging up. He'd rather call back than listen to that crap. He would have too if Susannah hadn't come in waving her shorthand notebook.

"I've got everything there is on the Krueger place."

"Andrew called from there. He wants you to pick him up."

"Pick him up?"

"His car's been stolen."

She dipped her head and looked at him, seemingly sure he was kidding her. It did sound like a bad joke.

"He thinks he found the murder weapon. Look, why don't we both go."

"And leave the office unattended?"

"That's how I found it."

"For once I anticipated Andrew. I know that sooner or later he would have asked me to check out the plat book, the back issues of the *Dealer*, whatever."

"You can tell me what you found on the drive."

She shook her head. "You can listen when I tell Andrew."

Whatever her news, it could scarcely compete with what Andrew had found. At the Krueger house, Andrew opened the neck of the duffel bag and let them look inside. They mustn't touch. He didn't want anything touched until Hanson had a crack at the contents of the bag.

"And the bag. It's amazing what they can do."

"Susannah's been checking out this house."

Andrew looked puzzled. "At the courthouse," she explained.

They helped themselves to the late Willard Palmer's bar and got comfortable. Hanson was flying up in one of the IBI's executive jets and expected to be there within the hour. Meanwhile, they could listen to what Susannah had found.

The plat book went back to Benjamin Harrison's authorization of the sale of Indian land, the eventual Krueger property having originally been part of a vast purchase by the Weems family, to whom the town of Wyler traced its origin. It had been Weems Junction before it was Wyler, Wyler having married a descendant of Weems and, as lieutenant governor, at the time more estimable than the departed Weems. Wyler had built up his fortune by selling land and it was from him that Krueger had purchased his 150 acres, which must have seemed an enormous plantation to the German immigrant. Krueger had worked the land for forty years before leaving the area.

"That's in the plat book?"

"No, Andrew. That's from the newspaper."

"Who did Krueger sell to?"

"The next owner of record is Emil Doremus."

"Doremus! He never farmed."

"He only bought it five years ago, just months before he died. He had been the rental agent since Krueger left."

Krueger had left in the early forties. If Doremus got title to the property only five years ago, he had to buy it from someone.

"Mary Margaret Ryan," Susannah read from her pad.

"Who's she?"

"The plat book doesn't say. None of the recorded papers say. She had a Pennsylvania address."

"Obviously an heir. Ryan. That's odd."

"Why?" Gerald asked.

"It's one of those things you have to know when you grow up in a place; maybe Dad told me. Krueger was fiercely proud of being German. When you think of it, the two world wars must have been hard on German-Americans. The thought that his property would end up with a woman with an Irish name has its ironies."

"I see what you mean," Gerald said, and Andrew looked at him as if he doubted it.

"If she's an heir, she must have Krueger blood."

"But think of all those Celtic genes disturbing the mix."

"Andrew, you can't possibly know Krueger felt that strongly about it."

"You mean I can't prove he did. Gerald, did you report my car missing?"

Gerald went to the phone and dialed the number he had stuffed into his pocket when that recorded music had begun.

"I couldn't reach them before we left."

"Couldn't reach the state police?"

Gerald extended the phone toward Andrew. He had been put on hold again and the awful music was audible. But even as he held the phone out, the music stopped. Gerald spoke into the phone.

"I want to report a missing automobile."

"Stolen," Andrew corrected.

"The owner thinks it was stolen."

He gave the description, covered the phone while Susannah gave him the tag number, then passed that on as well. How long had the car been missing?

Gerald handed the phone to his uncle. This was ridiculous, running errands for Andrew when he was right there in the room.

Gerald did not wait for Hanson to arrive, although he was reluctant to leave Susannah and Andrew stranded at the farm. He was even more reluctant to break his late afternoon golf date with Julie.

"Keep all this under your hat for now, Gerald."

"I won't even tell Glen Olson."

"Don't. I want the satisfaction of telling him with Grmzchak present. Hanson too if I can arrange it."

"He'll just go back to the Sanchez indictment."

"I'll ask for a dismissal."

"On what grounds?"

"A prosecutorial campaign against our client."

★

September was arguably the best month of the year to golf in Wyler. Old-timers at the country club considered summer over after Labor Day. There could be an Indian summer of tropical proportions, but the strawhats and white shoes, the garb of summer, would already be in storage. Golf too, being a summer sport, ended with Labor Day for such purists. Which was fine with Gerald.

The courses in Wyler, two of them, were tournament-quality. Unfortunately, that attracted people to them. Members were constantly showing them off to floods of guests and a round could be a slow thing in July and early August. But September was glorious.

Julie was waiting for him on the first tee, her

practice swings attracting attention not simply because of expertness of execution but because the body
executing the swing was something to behold. And
even more to be held. Gerald put a possessive arm
around her waist and kissed her cheek.

"Aren't you the bold one." Drops of perspiration
stood on her upper lip to almost erotic effect.

"I can get bolder."

"You already have rocks in your head."

"Ho-ho."

"Want to flip to see who goes first?" Julie always
played the men's tees.

"I'd love to flip you for it."

"Don't laugh. I'm going to whip you tonight."

"Not until after we golf."

She turned away to conceal her smile and bent to
tee up her ball. From that moment on she was all
business; but the more competitive the game, the
more amorous the sequel. Watching her drive rise
and carry over two hundred yards on the fly, Gerald
knew this was going to be a most competitive round.

ELEVEN

There was a delay of at least one day before the out-of-town newspapers were put on display in the St. Paul Public library. Gunther waited impatiently, but after a single glancing mention of Wyler in the Indianapolis paper, there was nothing further. He tried to get his mind off the farm, but the Krueger ledger he carried with him was a constant reminder of what he was engaged upon. He could not stop himself from imagining what might be going on in the backyard of the farmhouse. It would be just his luck for the police or a septic tank service or the telephone company to stumble upon that buried fortune. But if that happened, it would be on all the wire services immediately. Gunther could imagine what spin would be put upon the fact that all those investments were in German companies.

He took the train to Milwaukee, but was still not close enough to get news of Wyler. Chicago was no better. He ended up in Indianapolis, which had been his first point for staging operations; he stayed there long enough to catch up on news from Wyler. He decided it was time to return.

When he walked from his hotel to Meridian Rental, it was all he could do not to burst into song. Maybe the Horst Wessel song, just for the hell of it. He hadn't felt this good since everything had gone according to plan and he pulled out of the Wyler Oasis, mission accomplished. The sleazy rental agency was a mile away and Gunther walked with measured step, savoring what lay ahead. The interstate would sweep him along, almost too fast; after nearly two weeks of keeping himself away from Wyler—away from the scene of the crime, it occurred to him—he would at last be returning.

He imagined leaving another rented car in the same parking lot at the Wyler Oasis and retracing his steps of that fateful afternoon: over the trestle, up the hill to a point where he could look down at the house, perform at least in his head the act of triangulation described in the ledger and pinpoint where old Krueger had buried what he could not then have supposed would become unimaginable wealth. Gunther had, of course, verified with a broker that prewar Farben and Krupp stock was redeemable in subsequent issues or in cash. The broker could not keep the curiosity from his voice. Did Gunther possess such stock?

"I'm advising someone."

"By seeking advice. Wise man. If I can be of any further help . . ."

"Of course."

He made it sound like a promise, pocketed the eagerly given card, shook the broker's damp hand, and left. That had been in Paterson.

In Indianapolis, catching up in the library on events in Wyler, Gunther was irked to read of the arrest of a local farmer. The man's name invited dark thoughts. Glen Olson? How could they imagine Olson had done it? Nothing in the *Wyler Dealer* account gave a remotely plausible reason for the indictment, except that Olson seemed to be a favorite target of the county prosecutor. Grmzchak! What the hell kind of a name was that? You had to be constipated even to pronounce it.

No doubt it helped to know that Olson had not done it, but Gunther felt insulted too. He had planned the shooting as a mystery killing that would always remain unsolved. Out of the blue, without apparent warning or motive, a man is shot down in his backyard. If the police found anything, it would simply bear out what they already knew. Someone had been lying on the hillside waiting to shoot Willard Palmer, but they already knew that. They would never be able to connect him with the shooting. How could they? But he had not dreamt they would accuse someone else.

When he rented a car at Meridian Rental, he used his own name; but if the gum-chewing girl behind the desk (wearing a headset and obviously tuned out of the real world) make any connection between the

Franklin Meecham of two weeks before and Gunther Kunz, the movement of her jaw and the vacant look in her made-up eyes did not reveal it. He paid in cash as he had before. Meridian Rental was 102nd in the business and not trying very hard to better its rank. Try to deal in cash with Hertz or Avis or even Economy. Theirs was a totally plastic world, and Gunther was not supplied with credit cards in names other than his own. The girl turned to point out the window to where the car was, and in following the direction of her finger Gunther saw the envelope tacked to a bulletin board next to the window.

It was as if his eyes had zooming capacity, leaping across the room, magnifying the printed letters. FRANKLIN MEECHAM. Gunther knew five seconds of absolute terror, and when it passed, he realized for the first time the gravity of what he had done. For the first time he realized that despite his precautions he could be apprehended and if he were, he would go to prison for an inconveniently long time. At his age even a comparatively short sentence would be equivalent to life. And there were no short sentences for murder.

A jingling sound snapped him out of it. The girl had extended the keys to him and then shaken them when he did not respond. He thanked her, stepped away from the counter, and then looked over the maps displayed in a rack. The girl and the counter were reflected in the dusty window. She was paying no attention to him. Sin boldly, Luther had advised. Gunther bounded to the door, pulled it open, snatched the envelope from the board, and dashed through the mist to the Ford he had been assigned. His back prickled as he moved, and the envelope, in his inside jacket pocket now, seemed to press against his heart, making breathing difficult.

The car did not leap into life, but he pumped the gas a few times and then the engine roared. He pulled out of the Meridian driveway and almost immediately into the Big Boy restaurant next to it. In the men's room, behind the locked door of a stall, he took out the envelope and ripped it open.

Dear Cougar.
Congratulations! Your
secret is safe with me. Don't
worry about the bag. Any
reasonable reward will do.
Leave a note where you found this. Yorel.

It was printed with a soft-leaded pencil on a not very clean piece of paper. The envelope bore the printed legend of MERIDIAN RENTAL. An inside job? He found it difficult to think clearly. It was the one thing he was vain about, his mind, his calm clear Teutonic mind, but now it was a riot of thoughts.

He had been discovered! That was the inescapable fact. He had been observed executing his supposedly perfect plan and was now at the mercy of the idiot who had printed this note. He crumpled it up, wanting to cast it from him, throw it in the toilet and flush it to where it belonged. But, of course, he couldn't do that.

He squeezed his eyes shut and forced himself to

regain composure. Had he been watched taking the envelope from the board? To do that was to identify himself. Perhaps the one who had seen him shoot Palmer had watched him take the note. The girl? Bah. Someone could have been sitting in one of the dozens of parked cars in the lot, unseen, watching. He could have been recognized even before he took the envelope, but that would have sealed it.

How had the writer of the note found out he had rented the Cougar as Franklin Meecham? Again he thought of the girl. She was implausible enough to be plausible. It was the only lead he had. It was imperative that he gain the upper ground with this tormentor. The plan formed easily in his mind (plans always did), and after he turned it over and found nothing obviously wrong, he left the men's room.

He detoured through the kitchen, out the back door and dashed for the empty lot ten yards away. He cut through to the opposite street, spotted a Catholic church and went inside. The mist had turned to rain. Good. The church smelt of stale incense and burning wax. He lit a vigil lamp but did not pay for it. An offering to Thor.

Outside, he stood in the shelter of the church door, shirt open at the collar, the jacket taken from Lost and Found at the back of the church too small, binding him under the arms. The discomfort seemed a small price to pay for a change of identity. He had taken everything from his sports jacket before leaving it in Lost and Found. The hat was better, big even for his big head and, when he set off, provided him some protection against the rain.

Back at Meridian Rental he found an unlocked car in the back row that gave him a good view of the office and the girl behind her counter. He settled down to wait. In comfort. What was a BMW doing on the Meridian Rental lot? He hadn't seen a luxury car like this on the list from which he'd selected a car. Strange.

TWELVE

Driving the VW van into a ditch had been offering a hostage to misfortune, Leroy thought. Going like a bat out of hell toward Indianapolis, the driving effortless in the beautiful BMW that Mr. Andrew Broom had contributed to their departure—along with a wallet full of money and credit cards—Leroy made up his mind that he wasn't going to let Broom's car be a great big arrow pointing to Marilys and himself. To abandon it on a street, or just about anywhere else, was to guarantee it would be found soon; once found, it would tell whoever was interested where its borrowers had recently been.

Where do you put a car so it won't be found? His thought in Wyler with the van had been to find some secluded spot and put it there. Stupid. If you want to hide sand, you take it to the seashore. The challenge was to find the automobile equivalent of the seashore. Which, it dawned on him, was where they were headed.

Indianapolis. He would put the BMW in long-term parking at the Indianapolis airport and he and Marilys would take a bus to town and check out Meridian Rental. Maybe in reverse order. But he hummed happily at the thought of the BMW parked where it wasn't going to attract anyone's attention for a very long time.

They cruised by Meridian once or twice before Leroy turned in at the restuarant next to it. A guy at the counter at Meridian meant Marilys would go in and try to sweet-talk him out of information about a Cougar rented two weeks ago. A girl, and Leroy would have drawn the assignment.

"How'm I going to get him to tell me, Leroy?"

"When you ask me how to walk with a hitch in your getalong, I'll answer that question."

She punched his arm and got out of the car. She put a lot of motion in the way she walked up the street to the rental agency, for Leroy's benefit, but a couple of horns went off from the drive-in restaurant in admiration. Twenty minutes later she was back, wearing a funny smile.

"Already?"

"He hired me!"

"To do what?"

"Le-roy! To work behind the counter, renting cars, eight-hour shift, twice minimum wage."

"You asked him for a job?" Leroy was thinking of what happened to her the last time she was gainfully employed.

80

"He just took it for granted I was answering an ad."

"When do you start?"

She turned his wrist to read his watch. "An hour and fifteen minutes. That's why he hired me, I said I could start tonight."

"Good girl."

"What you going to do with this car?"

"Drive my girl to work in it."

"Let's rent the motel first."

Marilys stood under the shower like she'd taken root; Leroy practically had to pull her out of there.

"You want to pucker all over, girl?"

"Let's."

He chased her around the unit, snapping a towel at her bottom, but she didn't want to do anything before she went to work.

"Let's save that till I get home."

"I wasn't thinking of wearing it out."

After running around the room bareass naked almost since they got there, Marilys withdrew demurely to dress. They ate at the drive-in next door, and Leroy told her he'd come by once she got started and the boss left.

After driving around a couple of times, Leroy found an empty space in the back row of the Meridian lot that might have been waiting for the BMW. Leroy put it away and went among the parked cars toward the brightly lit little building. Marilys, in a red uniform, was pretty as a picture behind the counter.

"You got a four-cylinder Lincoln Continental for rent, lady?" he asked when he went in.

"I'll have to see your driver's license, sir. Will this be cash or credit?"

Marilys looked like she'd been behind that counter most of her life instead of fifteen minutes.

"I don't suppose you had a chance to check where the records might be."

"Leroy, I haven't a clue."

"Show me how you do it."

"I said later." She was making a joke. With Marilys you were never sure until she laughed.

"I meant show me your routine."

"You keep insulting me and you might wait forever."

The procedure was simple in one way, complicated in another. What a lot of paper went into renting a car! The form that went through the computer produced three copies as well as storing the data. That's what Leroy wanted to know. As soon as they knew how to call up what the computer had in storage, they would know who rented the Cougar.

Meanwhile, Leroy would go back to the motel. Marilys would keep the job until she learned how to find out about the Cougar.

"What'd you do with the BMW?"

"Parked out in your lot."

"It'll stick out like a sore thumb."

"Who will notice?"

"Someone may want to rent it."

"Don't rent it."

"When I'm not on."

"They can't rent it if it's not registered with the company."

He left the keys in the BMW. That way he felt he

had really abandoned it. The lot of Meridian Rental was the place to stash it, that was for sure. There was neither a garage nor a servicing crew to stumble upon the luxury car. Eventually, it would be found, no doubt, but eventually seemed a long way off.

After two nights they were no closer than before. Marilys surprised herself by liking the job. It was boring, but she bought a Walkman so that she could fill her mind with heavy metal while she was on duty. Leroy had the sense he was losing her, as if the job was a rival. He did not like the thought at all.

"Let's forget about the Cougar and hit the road," he suggested. "We don't want to settle down in Indianapolis."

"Not right away. Funny. I kind of like working again. It's sort of like a vacation."

"Well, you don't get two weeks."

The third day she said he didn't have to get out of bed and come get her when she got off at 6 A.M. She could get back to the motel by herself. Leroy nodded. And brooded about it after they ate at the drive-in and she had walked, brisk and businesslike, no business with the rear end, up the street to Meridian Rental. He felt that she was walking out of his life.

Face it, he told himself, I'm an old man and she's a girl. She'll never really grow up. I'm probably the longest she's stayed with anyone, anyway. The thought grew on him that there was someone else.

Back at the motel he watched the fights on TV, a replay of the previous Thursday night, shown from one to three. With the television off, the motel room was a lonely place. Odd noises coming through the

83

walls, but the reassuring sound of passing traffic outside. The sound of traffic had become the Muzak of his life.

He slept maybe half an hour, forty-five minutes. At five he got up and drove the Ford he had borrowed from Meridian to the drive-in, which, like the rental agency, was a twenty-four-hour operation. Marilys got mainly turn-ins during her shift, people wanting to avoid another full day's rental. At this hour he could see the little office and Marilys in it. She had the earphones on and was swaying to the beat. He felt a wave of tenderness for her. He hated himself for spying on her, for suspecting her. But not enough to go back to the motel and forget it.

So he was there when she went out to the street at ten after six. Alone. He felt ashamed of himself. But, almost immediately, the BMW came out of the lot and crawled up beside her. Marilys stopped, talked to the driver, and then went slowly around the car and got in. Leroy was so stunned he forgot to start the Ford, and when he remembered, he was so flustered he flooded the engine. By the time he got into the street, the BMW was nowhere in sight.

He drove back to the motel, wondering what she would tell him when she came back. If she came back.

By the time noon came, he knew she wasn't coming back. There was no way in the world she could explain six hours. She knew that and didn't even intend to try. Leroy went out and bought a six-pack, but he felt too bad to drink. He settled for a Diet Pepsi from the machine outside and lay on the bed staring at the blank TV through the afternoon.

He could go back to Arizona and the Dairy Queen. Fat chance. His wife would be a damned fool to take him back. Besides, he was spoiled for that life now. The life he wanted involved Marilys. He would never find anyone else like her. What he felt like doing was drowning himself in the motel pool after writing a note that would break Marilys's heart. If she ever heard of it.

Just after six he drove the Ford past Meridian, half fearing he would see her in there in her red coat, headset on, swaying to the music. But the man who had hired her was behind the counter, looking none too happy. Leroy turned in and drove past the office with the lights off; the guy didn't even look up. Leroy decided to cut over to the drive-in and try to figure out what to do next.

The BMW was in the back row. He couldn't believe it. He went over to it and looked inside. Marilys was in back, shoved down on the floor behind the front seats, her blind, wide-open eyes looking right at him. In her mouth was stuffed the note he'd had her pin to the board in the office.

THIRTEEN

Hanson was not the type to exhibit his emotions, but it was clear enough to Andrew Broom that the man from the IBI regarded the duffel bag and its contents as the key that would unlock the mystery of Willard Palmer's murder. He carried the new evidence away on the same plane that had brought him. Andrew was now prepared to see the shooting of Willard as a challenging problem rather than as a threat to his client. Maxine Shapiro, of course, drew small consolation from the news that Andrew no longer considered the indictment of Olson a serious threat. Her concern was for her own late client.

"Then who did it?"

"Knowing who didn't do it is a first step."

"There are millions of people who didn't do it."

He told her about the duffel bag. Her earlier fear

that an old acquaintance of Willard's had flown to Indiana from New York expressly to shoot her client had diminished, then disappeared. Her speculation now bore on nameless assassins roaming the heartland of the country, intent on snuffing out the life of artists and other sensitive people. She took the duffel bag to confirm this hypothesis.

"The state bureau of investigation will be able to learn a lot from that bag and its contents."

"Don't fingerprints wash away?"

"The agent seemed delighted to receive the evidence."

But when Hanson telephoned, he did not speak first of the duffel bag. "We've found your car."

"Good. Where was it?"

"In Indianapolis. God knows when it would have been discovered but for one thing."

"What was that?"

"The body in the back."

"Body?"

"The dead body of a woman. She's been there for a few days. This attracted the manager of the rental agency whose lot it is."

"A dead body?"

"Murdered. Strangled with the wires of her headset. The radio was still on when she was found."

"Good Lord."

"Her name was Marilys Agamata."

"Don't know her."

"I didn't think you would. Can I see you in your office this afternoon?"

"Only if you have a report on the duffel bag."

"That's one of my reasons for coming."

"What are the others?"

"Would three o'clock be all right?"

The story Hanson had to tell would have seemed wholly incredible to Andrew if he had not formed such a high opinion of the man's practical wisdom. That the duffel bag, Andrew's BMW, and an abandoned van found a mile and a half out of Wyler should be links in the same chain strained one's credulity. The link was fingerprints. On the gun, in the BMW, in the VW van partially tipped into a ditch half a mile from the river. Unidentified, thus far.

"Anything further on the dead woman?"

"A deputy saw her and a man drive off in that van. He had just discovered marijuana in the van. She let the air out of the tires of his cruiser, and they got away."

"What does the man look like?"

Hanson produced a photocopy of the Identi-Kit the sheriff's office had done. A fat bald man with a beard. Middle-aged.

"They ditched the van, stole my car, and he killed her?"

"Maybe. She had been working in the rental agency where her body was found. It could have been anyone."

"Sure."

People sometimes were killed by strangers but not very often if they had a spouse or lover. It was Andrew Broom's hunch that the bald man with the beard had killed Marilys Agamata. It was only a matter of time before they caught him, but it was unlikely that they would find him where they found the woman. A car missing from the rental agency was found parked at the Amtrak station. He could have gone anywhere. Then again, he might have left the car there to make them think that. Against all experience, Andrew found himself thinking of a killer as shrewd and crafty. Most killers all but turned themselves in, they left so obvious a trail. Maybe they wanted to get caught, but maybe they were just plain dumb.

The M1 rifle in the duffel bag was the one used to shoot Willard Palmer twice. There was a button missing from a flap pocket on the right leg of the dungarees, where the field telephone was found. Palmer's killer could not be the fat man. Palmer's killer had been methodical, planning the shooting with care. The only prints he had left were on the field phone, as if he had picked it up again after removing his gloves. That and dropping the duffel bag in shallow water where there was too good a chance it might be seen were his only mistakes.

Hanson listened to Andrew develop these thoughts. "This other guy might have killed them both, the woman and Palmer."

"What was he doing in Indianapolis?"

"Maybe he stole your car."

"Then what were the man and woman doing in Indianapolis?"

The corners of Hanson's mouth dimpled briefly. "Maybe they were all in it together and there was a falling out over the woman, with tragic consequences for her. And maybe we better hold all this speculation until we arrest one or both of them."

Good idea. Andrew had not recognized the Identi-Kit drawing of the man. He looked at the photographs of the woman's corpse and shook his head. He was sure he had never seen her before. It was unnerving to think of these strangers hovering in the vicinity. In the vicinity of Willard Palmer's farm. It was in the parking lot of the interstate oasis just across the trestle bridge that the deputy had seen the man and woman and their van. The van was found later, abandoned on Palmer's side of the river, the same day that Andrew Broom's BMW, which had been parked in Palmer's drive, was stolen. Six days later it was found in Indianapolis with the woman dead in the back.

It was impossible not to connect them with the shooting of Willard Palmer. But who was the other man? He was the one who had lain on the hillside, waiting for Willard. The description of the driver of the van did not match the impressions made there on the hill.

After Hanson left, Andrew sat in the easy chair in one corner of his office. His eyes were on the southern horizon, visible from the massive windows at the side of his office high in the First Bank Building in downtown Wyler.

He had sat here with Gerald when he persuaded his nephew to do as he had done, eschew a career with a large urban law firm and practice in Wyler. He had assured Gerald that there was no facet of the law he would not eventually deal with in this small city. It was only that chaos was on a more manageable scale here The law, he thought, was the major means to tame the beast latent in all of us, ready to spring forth and wreak havoc on the community. Andrew felt that his point was being proven to excess of late. Glen Olson had been a small though interesting problem, but with the shooting of Willard Palmer it became clear that an unknown and deadly cast of characters had been at loose in the area. Two murders, somehow connected, bad enough in themselves, indicated a hidden, unknown script that very likely was far from being played out.

"You think one or both of the men will be back?" Gerald asked. He now sat in another of the chairs, a modernistic shell-shaped artifact that so conformed itself to Gerald's body that he seemed to be floating in air.

"Don't say that," Susannah protested. She sat on the edge of a rust-colored couch, wearing a beige dress cinched at the waist, very full skirt, with great ocher and black splotches. One elbow rested on her crossed knee and a just lit cigarette in her long fingered hand sent a thin wisp of smoke toward the ceiling. That the details of his wife's appearance should so impress themselves on him told Andrew that he was feeling particularly vulnerable.

"How is it connected with Willard Palmer? I sent a copy of the Identi-Kit by fax machine to Maxine Shapiro. Nothing. She never saw the fat man before, was certain it was no one Willard had known in New York."

"Who gets the farm?" Gerald asked.

Andrew looked at him. *"Cui Bono?* Good boy! The farm reverts to Mrs. Doremus, but what about his money? Get on it."

Gerald was pleased by the praise, but unclear what getting on it entailed.

"Willard Palmer's will, Gerald. We need to know who stood to benefit from Willard's death."

The answer, discovered the following day, would have discouraged a lesser man than Andrew Broom. Willard had left all his worldly goods to a haven for cats in Pompano Beach. This came as a surprise to the proprietor of the place, who shrieked in hysterical glee when Gerald conveyed the news.

FOURTEEN

Doremus Realty, Inc., was located in a new wing of the house that Martha and Emil had bought when they first married. This first venture into the local real-estate market had quite unexpectedly started them on the career that continued even now that Martha was a widow. The addition was designed in the same bungalow style as the original house—white siding, green shutters bracketing the windows, a trellis over the entrance of the walk that led between box hedges to the office door. The potential customer entered with reassuring small-town images already imprinted on his imagination.

Emil had become quite a student of the psychology of the potential buyer. The more he learned, the more fatalistic he had become.

"What we say or do has little, if any, influence on the decision ultimately taken, my dear. These things, like marriage, are in the hands of God."

Not that Emil had become passive and inert. The profounder his conviction of the unimportance of his efforts, the more energetic he became. Martha, in turn, marveled at the transformation that came over Emil when he dealt with those seriously considering a real-estate transaction. Within minutes he became a coconspirator with the client, determined to overcome the mysteries and pitfalls of the real-estate market. His knowledge was at their service. What else are friends for? He didn't say that, of course; he didn't have to. And it was effective because he really and truly meant it. That he should receive the handsome commission he did when a sale was made seemed to strike him as an unlooked-for bonanza. What did he need beyond the satisfaction of his clients?

He was, perhaps, a slightly comic figure. People did make fun of Emil, Martha knew that. She would have resented it if there had been malice in it, but there was none. Part of Emil's charm was that he threatened no one, provided an easy opportunity for benevolent condescension, and seemed unaware of the smiles his naïveté elicited. Martha had loved him with all her heart and soul.

There had been a little one long ago, a daughter born premature who did not see three months of life. Martha never conceived again. It was as if somehow, deep inside themselves, she and Emil had said no to other children. If others had come, they would have accepted them joyfully. But each bore the indelible memory of that fragile infant, fruit of their love, who with a little sigh had departed this vale of tears.

When Emil died, Martha felt her own life had come to an end as well, but she had not given way to despair. It was silly, she supposed, and she would certainly never mention it to anyone, but often she had the definite sense that Emil was communicating with her, telling her what to do, not allowing her to let the business go to pot. In the end, Martha did very well on her own.

The great albatross of long standing was the Krueger property. Martha had stopped hoping that Willard Palmer's death had not tied that beast of a farm around her neck once more. She had studied the convoluted agreement drawn up by Andrew Broom and there was no doubt about it. With the death of Willard, his statement of intent to purchase two years from the date of the agreement was null and void. Martha Doremus, for all practical and legal purposes, was once more the proprietor of the Krueger property.

Whatever depression and resentment the thought entailed were mitigated when Andrew stopped by and told her of the bequest to the haven for cats.

"Cats!"

"Stray cats."

"I had no idea he was fond of cats."

"He loved them. But he was allergic to cat fur and couldn't keep one as a pet. It was apparently to make up for that deprivation that he had decided to provide for homeless cats."

"He seemed perfectly sane to me, Andrew."

Andrew was a fine figure of a man and his laughter was contagious. Martha felt she had just said something very witty.

"If I read your agreement correctly, Andrew, I am once more in possession of the farm."

"Congratulations."

She just looked at him. It would not do, of course, to tell him what a heartache that property had been. For so many years, Emil had simply rented it, having despaired of overcoming the local superstitions about the house. It was the backward farmer indeed who could not conquer whatever fears he might have in favor of those productive acres. But renting was one thing, purchase another. Willard Palmer had been the first real bite in years and Andrew had seemed intent on making it all but impossible to land him. Well, it was water over the dam now.

"Will you sell it?"

"Would you like to buy it?"

His shrug surprised and encouraged Martha but she proceeded gingerly.

"There are people who would be afraid to buy that house."

"Because of what happened to Willard?"

Dear God, it had not occurred to her that now the house was twice cursed. Abandoned by its builder and now the scene of a violent murder.

"A lot could be done for the place, Andrew. Not that it isn't in top condition. As you well know."

Oh, the repairs she had done before Andrew would let Willard Palmer put pen to paper. The Krueger property was a constant drain, requiring maintenance, insurance, the odd repair bill. It would be a sound business decision to give it away.

"It's not for us, Martha. I wish it were. The house has character."

"I wonder if I shouldn't just donate it to the county."

Another laugh, but his eyes never left hers. "Now that might anger a person or two."

"Oh?"

"Your heirs, Martha. I needn't explain mortality to you."

"I wish I had heirs, Andrew."

"No family?"

"Not in this world."

"But everyone has someone, Martha. Believe me, as a lawyer I can assure you of that. When there is property to inherit, people come out of the woodwork."

"Well, none will come out when I die, Andrew."

"But you have a will?"

"Andrew Broom soliciting legal business? I never thought to see the day."

He took it as the joke she intended it to be. And went on to tell her his thinking about the Willard Palmer murder.

"It is invariably a good basis for investigating a violent death, Martha. Who benefits from it?"

"And you think my imaginary heirs came and bumped off Willard Palmer so that when I go they would have the Krueger farm."

"I won't instruct you on the attractiveness of real estate. People have killed for far less."

"Andrew, if you can find someone who wants the farm that much, send them to me."

He accepted her offer of tea and the talk turned to other matters, Susannah mainly. Martha had known Susannah since she was a girl and had not been wholly convinced that marriage to Andrew was a wise thing for Susannah. How good it was to learn that she had been utterly and completely wrong. It was perfect for both of them. Certainly for Andrew. Not that Martha could imagine marrying again herself. If Emil had survived her and remarried, she was sure her heart would have broken in her grave. But Andrew's first wife had been . . . well, speak well of the dead.

That night, knitting squares for an afghan, from time to time following a program on television over her half-glasses, Martha thought again of Andrew's question. Who benefited from the death of Willard Palmer? It came down to asking who would be interested in the Krueger farm being available again, and as she had not quite said to Andrew, the answer to that was nobody.

Franklin Meecham.

Her breath caught. She had not remembered that phone call from the Baltimore lawyer. Who did not exist. But the telephone call had been real. The inquiry had been made. It was something to take such comfort from as she could.

There might be one person in the world who would like to own the Krueger farm.

If only he would call again.

She had half a mind to take out ads in the Baltimore and Indianapolis papers. Whoever Franklin Meecham was, he might see them and be glad to know that the property he had expressed such interest in was once more on the market.

FIFTEEN

Gunther checked into a motel thirty miles south of Wyler, showered for fifteen minutes, took a sleeping pill, and got into bed. He did not fall asleep. Or perhaps he fell asleep and dreamt he was awake. He spent four restless hours, staring up at the stippled ceiling, trying to make his mind as blank as the expanse above him.

Killing the woman at Meridian Rental had been a mistake, a grievous mistake. He was guilty of hubris, the fatal step over the line. Would he suffer for it? It was because he felt he was less vulnerable awake than asleep that he lay there, open-eyed, bargaining with the universe to let him off easy just this once.

Although a mistake, the killing was understandable, was it not? Imagine anyone connected with that girl daring to blackmail him. More seriously, the penciled note meant that all his elaborate planning was rendered ridiculous. But when could he have been seen? How could anyone have known of that duffel bag in the river?

The thin, big-breasted girl with eyes that held a hundred secrets she would not divulge to Gunther looked at him in contempt when he asked who had left the note pinned to the board in the agency office.

"He asks me to get in contact with him."

"Leave a note."

He had waited for her shift to end, hoping the author of the note would come for her, but at this ungodly hour of the morning that seemed unlikely. Her replacement arrived and he had the BMW purring like a kitten when she started out to the street. Imagine leaving the keys in that car—but of course it didn't belong to Meridian Rental. He slid up beside her. Her face lit up at the sight of the car.

"Can I give you a ride?"

She bent and saw who it was and shook her head.

"Don't you remember me from Wyler?"

That stopped her, but didn't seem to alarm her. "No."

"Get in. I'll take you home. Yorel asked me to."

One side of her mouth went up in a smile and she scooted around the car and got in. He pressed the button on the door beside him, locking her in, and accelerated into the street. The speed threw her back against the seat, and when he swung to the left she lost her balance again and rolled toward the door. Her head hit with a bang and she was silent.

Ten minutes later, when she came to, he had her wedged on the floor behind the front seat. He himself sat in the backseat, his stocking feet pressed into the small of her back. The girl groaned and he increased the pressure on her back.

"Who is Yorel?"

"Go to hell."

"He asks me to get in touch with him."

She told him again to write a note and he drove his heel into her side. She gasped in pain. He did it again, feeling an odd pleasure in her pain. She represented the failure of his plan, insofar as nothing he did in Wyler was supposed to tell anyone who he was. Her willingness to come with him when he mentioned the name on the note made it clear that she was part of the attempt to blackmail him. She would learn that the stakes are high when one interferes with Gunther Kunz. High indeed. He looped the wire of her Walkman around her neck and, keeping his feet on her back, levered her head up. She was wedged tightly in between the back and front seats and could not move.

"Do you want to die?"

Her eyes rolled toward him, filled with hatred. He tugged on the wire and she gagged. He eased up.

"Where can I find him?"

He let all the tension out of the wire so she could speak. She took the opportunity to invite him to commit an obscene act. Angrily, he jerked at the wire and she began to choke. It was to stop the noise that he increased the pressure. Eventually, she was quiet. She was dead.

"Now why did you do that?" he asked aloud. He thought he was addressing the girl. As the day wore on, he realized he was asking himself.

He returned to Meridian Rental, drove past the office, and put the BMW back where it had been. He reached over the seat and stuffed the note into her mouth.

The man in the office was paying no attention to the parking lot. He was on the phone, standing, in profile, babbling at a great rate into the instrument. Gunther slipped out of the BMW, bent over, and moved toward the drive-in restaurant next door.

He rented a car from Hertz and drove to the motel, where he could not sleep. He should not have killed the girl. He had done it out of pique. Palmer had been entirely different, a means to an end; killing him had been a rational choice. What did killing the girl accomplish? As for the man, Yorel, two things could happen. Either, finding the girl dead and taking the note to be a warning, he would flee as fast as he could go. Or, enraged by what was found in the backseat of the BMW, he would vow to track down Gunther if it was the last thing he did. Gunther rather thought the man would do the first.

After he left the motel and continued north, the sleeping pill took effect and he had to pull into a rest area, where he slept for hours. The sun had set and passing cars had their headlights on when he awoke. His tongue was furry, his head cloudy. He felt a strong temptation to crawl into the backseat and go to sleep again. A newly acquired aversion to backseats

103

caused him to start the car and drive, yawning, back into traffic.

In Wyler, at the Hoosier Towers, he slept until ten-thirty the following morning. After breakfast, with the aid of a city map, he drove to the address of Doremus Reality, Inc.

The office doorbell was not answered. Gunther went to the door of the house proper and fared no better. No car in evidence, the garage door was locked. He should have telephoned first, perhaps, but he had not wanted to run the risk of her recognizing his voice. He wrote a note—printed it, actually—and put it under the office door. In it he told her to call him at the Hoosier.

He did not relish the thought of just wasting time until Mrs. Doremus came back. Who knew how long she might be gone? If she were with a client, it could be hours. For all he knew, she was not even in town. Again he had the sinking feeling that all his careful plans to acquire the Krueger property were unraveling.

He drove east and west, north and south, on the downtown grid of streets, as if he were playing tic-tac-toe. That the Krueger farm could be reached in a matter of minutes occurred to him and he knew he would go there. It was foolish, more foolish than killing that girl, but he knew he would do it. All he could hope to do was postpone it. Still full of his breakfast, he stopped at a restaurant, where he was early for lunch.

"Something from the bar?" The waitress weighed two hundred pounds, her skirt was too short, but she moved with an odd lightness on her little feet.

"Manhattan," he said, not believing his ears.

"On the rocks?"

"Yes."

On the rocks indeed. What was he doing having a drink at ten minutes of twelve? But when it came, he sipped it with pleasure. It no longer seemed further evidence that he was acting crazily. Have a drink, relax. Of course. It was the sweet vermouth that won his allegiance. He would have ordered that alone if he had thought. Next time.

Next time? But he did reorder and, rather than confuse the waitress, had another manhattan. The restaurant was filling up and he ordered.

"The special is swiss steak."

Not on your life. He hated the smug Swiss with their record of profitable neutrality.

"Let me have a hamburger."

She drew his attention to the embarrassment of choice he had among the many hamburger offerings. He asked for the simplest one. He took a bite or two of it and that was all. He had left half his second manhattan, for dessert. He tossed it off and took his check to the register. As he was leaving, he looked back and saw the betrayed look on the fat waitress. He stopped, nodded, and then went back and lay a dollar on the table where he had eaten.

"Thank you, sir. Have a nice day."

Have a nice day! In Bavaria they said *"Gruss Gott"* with equal meaninglessness.

"I intend to," he replied.

"Good!"

He wondered what it would be like to strangle her.

105

★

In the end, he sped past the Krueger farm, hardly glancing at the house as he went by. A mile up the road he turned around and came back slowly. The very spatial coordinates seemed to reach out and claim him as he neared the house. Directly in front of it, knowing he was within fifty yards of the fortune old Krueger had hidden there, he felt suffused with a sense of destiny. That house would soon be his and with it the buried certificates that would enrich him and vindicate the old German.

★

Mrs. Doremus looked puzzled when he mentioned his note.

"I put it under the door."

She looked down, opened and closed the door again, lifted the mat. No note.

"It only asked you to call me at my hotel," he explained.

"And what can I do for you?"

"First I must tell you what a lovely town you have."

"I couldn't agree more," she said with delight.

"You're a native?"

"I am indeed."

"Been in the real-estate business a long time?"

"My husband and I started this business longer ago than I like to remember."

"Then there are two of you."

"Oh, Emil's dead."

"I'm sorry."

Her eyes filled suddenly with tears, and Gunther was about to put his arm about her but stopped himself. Beware of weeping widows. He decided that her tears were a good omen. When he sat across the desk from her, he was certain she would never connect him with phone calls from Franklin Meecham.

"So you're moving to Wyler."

"I hope I'm doing the right thing."

"You certainly are. Are you retired, Mr. Kunz?"

He had given her his right name. He was embarking on the final phase of his plan and there was no reason not to identify himself correctly.

"That's what they tell me."

She smiled. "Is it an apartment you want, or a house?"

"An apartment would make more sense, but I can't stand living in such proximity to people. There's no choice in a large city, of course."

"There is a far larger selection of houses than apartments in Wyler. You'll want a small house, I suppose."

"I'm not so sure. I don't like being cramped either. And I would want a large lot. A very large lot. What's the point of moving to the Midwest if you can't enjoy the space?"

"I have half a mind to show you some country places."

"Country places?"

"Not too far out. I'm sure we could find something

that would suit you in town, but I wouldn't close my mind to a place in the country if I were you."

"I am in your hands, Mrs. Doremus."

And so it was that he was let into the Krueger house for the first time and walked through the rooms he knew so well from the floor plans in the ledger.

"It's already furnished?"

"All this can be moved out. I just don't like the house empty."

"Move it out? But I like it just as it is. What's the price?"

"It's listed at seventy-nine thousand."

"Good Lord!"

"That's a very reasonable price."

"Reasonable? I should say it is. Can we see the rest of the house?"

They spent two hours going through the place. Gunther showed relatively minor interest in the yard, except to say it set the house off well. He was afraid that, if he went into the backyard, he would fall on his kness and begin digging with both hands.

"I love it," he announced when they stood again in the living room.

"Good. Then I suggest we go back to the office and talk turkey."

At the office she brewed tea and Gunther accepted a cup. He offered $70,000 and she countered with $75,000.

"Done."

She beamed like a bride and extended her hand. He shook it. She assured him she would get the process started immediately.

108

"How will you be paying?"

"Cash."

Her smile grew even brighter. "Then we can move things right along. Have you any preference for a lawyer?"

"Whom do you usually use?"

She hesitated. "Andrew Broom."

"Then Andrew Broom let it be."

SIXTEEN

The only place Leroy knew to look for the sonofabitch in the Cougar was in Wyler. He would have liked to just go, forget all about it; nothing he could do would bring Marilys back. Besides, she was probably better off now than chasing around the countryside with an old bastard like himself.

Back at the motel, he stood in front of the bathroom mirror and could have cried at what he saw. Who in hell did he think he was, dressed like that, wearing that beard? He looked like a middle-aged man who thought he was still young. Marilys had made him feel young; but now he felt very, very old.

He could not close his eyes without seeing her contorted face, bulging eyes, the black tongue lolling from her mouth. His hand when he plunged it into his coverall pocket closed over the note he had pulled from her mouth.

110

"I'll kill the sonofabitch," he told his reflected self. "I'll find him and I'll kill him."

A shrewd look entered his mirrored eyes. He would track the bastard down but not looking like this. He went into the room and got Marilys's scissors—shears, she had called them—and back in the bathroom began to snip away at his beard. When he got it down to stubble, he lathered up and carefully shaved his face clear. His beardless face made it obvious he needed a haircut too. Well, he'd get one. And some different clothes.

When he went to the motel office, he was greeted like a stranger. He said he was moving out.

The kid looking after the office had a long neck in which a prominent Adam's apple slid up and down. His nose was long and bony and seemed to wear his eyes as if they were pince-nez.

"Moving out?"

"Leroy White."

"Jesus, what happened? I didn't recognize you."

"I shaved."

"Why? You look like hell. What's the missus think of it?"

He meant Marilys. Leroy did not want to tell the kid Marilys was dead. He shrugged.

"Ain't she seen you yet?"

"How much do I owe you? I paid up Friday, but I don't want to pay for a whole 'nother week."

"Let me figure it out."

"I'll be back."

But three minutes later there was a knock on the unit door and when Leroy opened it, it was

111

the kid. He looked up at Leroy with a knowing grin.

"What'd she say?"

"Get the hell out of here."

"Hey, missus, how you like him with his bare naked face?"

Leroy hit him on the side of the head, sending him spinning sideways. He lost his balance and dropped to a sitting position with a jolt. He looked at Leroy, startled, accusing, hurt.

"Why'd you have to do that?"

"How much do I owe?"

"I was just kidding around."

"I know. It's all right."

"You think it's all right, huh? Haul off and hit a guy but it's all right."

"I'm not going to say I'm sorry, kid. Give me the bill."

He took it inside and closed the door. It was not going to be easy to leave. The place was haunted with Marilys. Standing at the foot of the bed, looking at her side of it, he began to cry, sobs shaking his body. When the first wave was over, he kept it up, forcing it a little. He had forgotten how pleasant it was to cry.

The kid took the money in silence, but he looked past Leroy to the car and its empty passenger seat.

"I'm going to pick her up at work," Leroy said to no one in particular.

The kid ignored him, handing back the change.

"You want a receipt."

"Yeah. Give me a receipt."

What the hell did he want a receipt for? It was like hitting the kid again, asking for a receipt.

Then he headed for Wyler, driving the Meridian Ford that Marilys had checked out to Andrew Broom.

★

He lucked out when he drove through downtown. Coming out of an underground garage was the sonofabitch. Leroy stopped and waved the guy into traffic, then cozied up behind. He wasn't going to let him get away now.

He parked up the street when the Cougar stopped at the real-estate office. In the rearview mirror, Leroy watched him give up on the office door and go to the entrance of the house. No luck. He wrote something then, using the top of his car for a desk, and went up to the office door and stooped over. He wasn't carrying the piece of paper when he went back to his car.

Leroy leaned over when the man drove past his parked car and, when he was out of sight, went back to the realtor's office and pulled the note out from under the door. Asking a realtor to phone him at a downtown hotel. Leroy could put two and two together. That meant he wanted to buy here and Leroy thought he knew the place the man wanted. And now the man had a name. Gunther Kunz. Leroy tried the name for size, saying it with a sneer. "Okay, Gunther baby, now you're going to get yours."

Not that Leroy was in any hurry. He didn't intend to rush into this. Gunther had killed two people that

Leroy knew of, and he sure as hell didn't want to be the third.

Sticking with the tried and true, he went out the interstate and parked at the Wyler Oasis, on the side away from the river. He crossed through the restaurant to the other side of the interstate and in a minute was at the trestle. Out on it a third of the way, he stopped and looked down. The water was clear and shallow, but there was no sign of the duffel bag Marilys said she had pitched in. Anger welled up in him. If she were here, he'd swat her, he didn't care if she was dead.

He went on over the trestle then and up the hill, where he lay down and looked at the house. He had all the time in the world and he did not think he was waiting in vain. An hour and a half later, a car pulled in and Gunther and a little old lady got out. They went into the house and Leroy just lay there smiling. When they came out into the backyard, he stopped smiling and nodded.

Now he knew how he was going to pay back Gunther Kunz.

SEVENTEEN

Given a choice between going to court for the formalities of having the charges against Glen Olson dismissed or flying down to Indianapolis to fetch Andrew's BMW, Gerald did not hesitate.

"I assume I'll be paid by the hour."

"For getting a day off? Don't be ridiculous."

"Maybe I'll stay overnight."

Andrew, who had been consulting the computer installed behind his desk, turned and looked closely at Gerald.

"You don't intend to take anyone with you, I hope."

"My lips are sealed."

Andrew frowned. Gerald wished his suspicions were justified. The fact is, he would not dream of asking Julie to fly off to Indianapolis with him for an overnight visit. Affectionate as she occasionally allowed herself to be, and much as it looked as if their liaison could become permanent, Julie was impervious to the ultimate seductive weapon that feminism had put into the arsenal of the predatory male. It was not her idea of liberation to become the voluntary plaything of a man.

"If you should take someone on a trip involving the firm, I can be held liable for any accident."

"I'll be careful."

The frown deepened. Did Andrew really know him so little? When he was at his apartment packing for the trip, Andrew phoned.

"I'll drive you to the airport."

"That's not necessary."

"Noblesse oblige."

"That's what they tell me."

"I'll be by in ten minutes."

He might have teased Andrew more by saying he had already made arrangements. He couldn't say he was leaving his car in long-term parking, since he would not be flying back.

"That's very nice of you, Andrew."

"I'll be there."

"We'll both appreciate it," he said, but the phone had gone dead.

When they got to the airport, Andrew pulled up in front of the terminal and left his motor running.

"Make sure they've got all the bodies out of the car before you take possession of it."

A jolly thought. It stayed with him as the little Fairchild skipped over the clouds to Indianapolis. Once inside the terminal, Gerald was surprised to

116

hear his name being called over the PA system. He picked up a courtesy phone.

"This is Gerald Rowan."

"One moment, please."

He was given a number to call. It was Hanson at the IBI. He had telephoned Andrew to find that he was in court but had been told that Gerald would be in Indianapolis. Could Gerald stop by Hanson's office?

"I'm glad you could come," the agent said, handing Gerald a cup of coffee that looked as if it had been drained from a crankcase. "Some interesting developments."

The woman whose body was found in Andrew's car had been working at the rental agency in whose lot the car had been parked. More interesting, she had been living with a man in a motel a mile away from the agency. Not only did the man fit the description of the driver of the van and apparent thief of the BMW, his prints in the hotel unit confirmed that he was the same man.

"The girl had been with him in Wyler. She's the one who let the air out of the deputy's tires."

"A falling out among thieves?"

"That's how it looks. The clerk who was on duty when Leroy checked out—his name is Leroy White; at least that's how he registered—said he acted very strangely, pretended his wife was going with him. He had shaved off his beard. When the clerk took the bill to the unit, he was attacked by the man."

"Why?"

"The kid says he thinks Leroy was afraid he'd see that the wife wasn't around. That thought came later,

117

obviously. But he says Leroy had been acting strangely earlier when he came to the office."

"What was the point of putting the body in the BMW?"

"That's where she died. It would have been a matter of moving it."

The name he had used at the motel was that of a man who had deserted his family in Arizona, which is where the girl Marilys had been traced to. She had worked for Leroy White there in a Dairy Queen and apparently they had gone off together in her VW van. Since then the improbable couple—Leroy was probably twice her age—had driven aimlessly around the country.

"Any idea where he might have gone?"

"The car he left in belonged to Meridian Rental. It was signed out to Andrew Broom."

Hanson watched Gerald laugh as if it were a phenomenon he was seeing for the first time. Perhaps there weren't many laughs in the life of an agent for the IBI.

"Your uncle's wallet was stolen with the car. One of his credit cards was used at Meridian."

"But those were reported stolen. Why didn't the clerk check and find out?"

"The clerk was Marilys Agamata."

Gerald made a face. Of course. "But you can run a check on the car."

"Oh, it's already turned up."

"Where?"

"In Wyler. In the basement garage of the Hoosier Towers."

"Why in hell would he go back there?"

"I have given up trying to understand the motives of killers. The main thing is that we know his whereabouts."

Gerald checked the backseat and the trunk before getting into the BMW. It didn't help much. The realization that a woman had been strangled right behind the seat in which he sat had the effect of making the most comfortable car in the world uncomfortable. The girl and her middle-aged lover Leroy had driven this car from Wyler to Indianapolis. The tape in the machine might be one they had listened to on the trip. He pushed the play button and the nasal voice of Roger Miller filled the car. One of Andrew's favorites. He made no bones about liking country-western.

"I was into it before the rush," he insisted to Gerald. "It's getting more and more glitzy all the time. Tuxedos at the Grand Ole Opry." He shook his head. Blow-dried hair on the good old boys twanging their guitars and singing their story songs. Progress? Andrew saw it as decadence. He added fewer and fewer new albums to his cache, and the old ones became more precious to him. When Willie Nelson showed up on Johnny Carson with a shampooed beard and his bandana washed and ironed, Andrew declared it was the end. Country-western music was what he already owned. There would be no more. Roger was singing that sure as God made little green apples something or other in Indianapolis in the summertime. Maybe that song had determined Leroy and Marilys to head for Indianapolis.

When he tired of Roger Miller, Gerald switched to radio and eventually heard of the manhunt under way for Leroy White in connection with the murder of a car-rental clerk in Indianapolis. There was no mention of the car being found in Wyler.

Gerald drove past the Hoosier on his way to the office and was almost surprised that the block surrounding the parking garage wasn't cordoned off, police swarming all over the place. On impulse, he swung in, went down the ramp, and got his ticket from the automatic dispenser. For five minutes he went up and down the aisles of the garage. There were several cars with plates that were not local and might have been from Indianapolis. There were no police in evidence.

When he left, the attendant frowned at the ticket after punching it.

"It says you entered six minutes ago."

"Was it that long?"

"Something the matter?"

"I was going to ask you the same thing."

If she knew anything, she would never need acting lessons. "Fifty cents," she said.

The attendant in the parking garage of their building was delighted to have the BMW back. What would his reaction be if he know about the body?

"Where did they find it?" He was a boneless kid who spent all day slumped in a chair. Gerald doubted he could ever close his mouth over all those teeth.

"Indianapolis."

"Naw. When I steal it, I'll get a lot farther than that."

"Keep an eye on it, will you?"

"Are you kidding?"

"In Indianapolis someone stuffed a corpse in the back when nobody was looking. We don't want that happening here."

His mouth hung open more widely than usual.

EIGHTEEN

Dominic Grmzchak avoided looking Andrew in the eye as they advanced to the bench. The prosecutor informed Judge Bellicini that the charges against Glen Olson were being withdrawn in the matter of the death of Willard Palmer. Understandably, the judge wanted a reason.

"Insufficient evidence, your honor."

"As counsel for the defense argued in the first place, your honor."

Bellicini's liquid eyes, only half-visible because of the heavy purplish lids, rolled and rested on Andrew.

"I meant, your honor, that the state has precisely as much evidence now as before."

"What has changed?" Bellicini asked Grmzchak in a throaty whisper.

"Suspicion has fallen on someone else."

"Are you bringing charges against that someone else?"

"In due course, your honor."

"Is this other person in custody?"

"Not yet," Grmzchak said miserably.

Bellicini, in dismissing the charges, suggested to the prosecutor that the court had better things to do than to be manipulated in the prosecutor's vendetta against Glen Olson. Emboldened, Andrew asked for a dismissal of the charges against Olson in the Esteban Sanchez accident.

"Accident?" Bellicini drawled. "Isn't that what the trial is meant to determine?"

The court, in short, was not ready to admit twice in one day that it had made a fool of itself. Nonetheless, Andrew, picking up his briefcase and stuffing it with papers, felt that he had done his client much good.

"Are you bringing charges against Leroy White?" Grmzchak asked.

"For stealing my car?"

"I'd like to issue a warrant for his arrest."

"Go ahead."

"To establish a jurisdictional claim. I don't want Indianapolis trying to horn in."

"Why not indict him for the murder of Willard Palmer? The IBI can give you all the evidence you need. You've got a free track there now."

Grmzchak grimaced. Andrew didn't blame him, but the prosecutor could use a little salt in the wound. His zeal was getting the better of him. It would be a lot better all around for any trial to be held in

Indianapolis. Any defense lawyer would ask first thing for a change in venue if Grmzchak attempted to try a stranger for a capital offense in a town the size of Wyler.

"Martha Doremus called," Susannah said when he got back to his office. "She has a client for you."

Andrew wrinkled his nose. After the grief he had given Martha drawing up the agreement to purchase for Willard Palmer, he couldn't believe she wanted him involved in any more real-estate transactions. Was that why he had written such a protective document for Willard Palmer?

"Get her on the phone."

"No need to. I told her you'd be back from court before three."

Martha arrived five minutes later, buoyant and suppressing a smile. Andrew got her settled in an easy chair that enabled her feet to touch the floor. She smoothed her skirt demurely over her bony knees.

"I'm going to have tea, Martha. How about you?"

"I would love a cup of tea."

"Why don't you join us, Susannah."

"Yes, Susannah, do. I'll hold my news until you do."

Susannah had the tea things out in record time, her every move followed by the beaming approval of Martha.

"I have a buyer for the Krueger farm," Martha announced, the words bubbling out of her mouth. "He has seen it, he wants it, he will pay cash. I suggested to him that he employ your services. I'm here on his behalf."

"Well," Andrew said, "that is very good news."

Susannah handed Martha her cup and then kissed her on the forehead. "Congratulations."

A little frown flitted across Martha's forehead. "Now don't make it sound like too much of a triumph."

"Who's the eager buyer?"

"His name is Gunther Kunz."

"Where is he from?"

"The east. Paterson, New Jersey. He's anxious to get away from the crowded city."

A small warning went off in Andrew's head. His memory of Paterson was vague, but he did not think of it as a crowded metropolis.

"What does he do?"

"He's retired."

"From what?"

"You'll have to ask him for all these details, Andrew. You will forgive me if my interest focused on the fact that he wants to buy the Krueger farm."

"Did you tell him what happened to the previous owner?"

Martha did not look up from sipping her tea. "Not yet."

"Is he in town?"

"At the Hoosier."

"If he mentions the Krueger place to anyone, they'll sure as shooting tell him, Martha. It would be better if he heard it from you."

"I agonized about it, Andrew. I did." She looked imploringly at Susannah. "God knows what may have gone on in the houses I sell people. I'm not selling them that. I'm selling them a house."

Susannah put a hand on Martha's arm, saying

nothing. Susannah could express more in a gesture than others did in words.

"Susannah, get hold of Mr. Kunz at the Hoosier Towers and tell him I am at his disposal whenever he'd like to come. Preferably immediately." He said to Martha, "I'll get all the cards on the table at once."

Martha was looking at him as she had during the negotiations over Willard Palmer's agreement. She wondered why she'd come to Andrew.

"Martha, before Susannah makes that call, are you sure you want me handling this? I'll understand perfectly if you take it to someone else."

"Of course I want you!"

"Just remember that I will be representing the purchaser."

"Oh, I am quite aware of that, Andrew. And Doremus Realty is never looking for the easy way. We want the client's interests well represented."

Susannah, who had hesitated in the doorway, went off to place the call. While she was gone, Gerald came in, full of news. Susannah returned to say that Mr. Kunz was apparently not in his room, and everyone looked eagerly at Gerald; he told them about his day.

"What a bonus this is," Martha exclaimed when Gerald told of the identification of the girl's killer with the man she had been living with, the man whom she had been traveling with in the VW van and who was most likely the killer of Willard Palmer. "My buyer will feel much better with a mystery solved."

"Where is Leroy White now, I wonder," Andrew mused.

"Here."

Martha almost choked on her tea. Susannah asked Gerald if by here he meant Wyler.

"That's only a guess. He rented a car in your name, Andrew."

"Good heavens!" Martha cried, dabbing at her mouth.

For fifteen minutes more the four of them went over Gerald's day in Indianapolis. How Grmzchak's mouth would water at the prospect of Leroy White showing up in his jurisdiction. Once he laid hands on him, he would never let him go.

The phone rang and Susannah took it in her office. She looked in with her eyes widened significantly.

"It's a Mr. Gunther Kunz," she said.

Andrew took the call at Susannah's desk. "Andrew Broom speaking."

"Mr. Broom, my name is Gunther Kunz. Mrs. Doremus gave me your name."

"Yes, she told me that. In fact, she's here now."

"I had been speaking to her of a real-estate deal."

"If you want me to represent you, I will. In fact, if you would care to come over now, we could get started on it."

"I'm afraid I can't do that."

Andrew's heart sank. Someone must have told him of the sniper who had picked off Willard Palmer. "Mr. Kunz, before you decide anything, I think we should talk."

"There's nothing I'd like better. But you will have to come to me. I'm in the county jail."

127

"The county jail!"

"Some idiot arrested me at my hotel. He thinks I'm someone else. Someone called Leroy White."

"Oh my God."

"When I try to tell them who I am, they ask me if I'm sure I'm not really Andrew Broom. Will you come sort this out?"

"I'll be right there."

He looked into his office, where Martha and Susannah and Gerald were chattering away. It seemed a shame to say anything until he knew what was going on.

"I won't be gone long," he said cheerily.

"Where are you going?"

"Gunther Kunz has asked me to come see him."

"I can be reached at home anytime this evening," Martha said, a pleading tone in her voice. She clearly did not want to be on pins and needles for long.

"I'll call," he promised.

And then he hurried off to the county jail to see what Grmzchak had wrought this time.

NINETEEN

In the basement garage of the Hoosier Towers, Leroy attached the license plate from Meridian Rental onto the car Gunther Kunz had driven from Indianapolis. In the glove compartment he put the papers Marilys had filled out in the name of Andrew Broom. Cars moved past on the ramp behind him, noises echoed in the concrete cavern of the garage, but Leroy went about his work unhurriedly, calmly, deliberately. Before getting out of Gunther's car he wiped every surface he had touched. He had not gripped the steering wheel, and the prints found there would suffice to show that Gunther had indeed been driving this car. He put the last of the marijuana in the backseat, pushed down not quite out of view.

His work done, he walked slowly to the front of the garage and entered the office. On the huge glossy calendar behind the desk a nude girl wearing an abandoned look and nothing else was playing with a kitten. The man at the desk was smoking a cigarette in a stained plastic holder. It tilted upward in greeting.

"Can I use your phone?"

"There's a pay phone just outside."

"Thanks."

He asked to use the phone book, and while he studied it, the man went back to the well-thumbed magazine open on the desk before him. More nude girls, some with animals. There must be a technical name for a man interested in that sort of thing. Leroy plucked the card for Gunther's car from its pocket in the rack on the wall and pulled open the office door admitting a fresh smell of exhaust.

"Thanks."

The man growled in reply. He sounded like an animal himself. Maybe that was the punishment for his vice.

It was better in the booth, a sealed-off world where a little fan tried ineffectually to cool the air. He dialed 911. The voice that answered sound anxious.

"In the basement garage of the Hoosier Towers you will find the car that Leroy White drove from Indianapolis."

He hung up and walked out of the garage and down the sunny autumn street of Wyler, Indiana.

He did not go far. At the corner he crossed the street and sat on a bench an undertaker had provided for those awaiting the bus. How many who sat here thought, as Leroy did, that they were waiting for the undertaker as well? His eyes filled with tears as he thought of Marilys. What a rotten thing to do to her. Well, Herr Gunther Kunz would pay for what he had done, the price of his life, ultimately; but first, he must be harassed and made to realize what was happening to him and why.

He had been seated on the bench for five minutes and failed to board the two buses that stopped, their doors hissing open invitingly, when the sheriff's car arrived. At the wheel was the fat young man who had tried to arrest Leroy at the Wyler Oasis a hundred years ago. It seemed like at least a hundred years ago. Bad luck. He would be convinced by the car, Leroy was sure of it, but when he faced Gunther he would know that something was wrong. Or would he? Gunther, of course, would deny that he was Leroy White, despite all the evidence to the contrary in his car. A check on the license plate would reveal that he had rented the car in the name of Andrew Broom, and in the glove compartment would be found the Wyler lawyer's wallet containing the very credit card that had been used by Marilys when she rang up the bill. By then the deputy should be joined by others, and matters would go beyond what he did or did not remember of the man he had tried to arrest at the oasis.

And so it happened, more or less. The deputy came out of the garage on foot, ten minutes after having driven his cruiser down the ramp. He waddled to the entrance of the hotel and went through the revolving door just as the realtor drew up to the curb and let Gunther out. He leaned down to speak to the woman at the wheel of the car, turned, and went through the revolving door.

Leroy crossed his legs, put an arm over the back of the bench, and looked benevolently at the passing traffic. He was almost used to being beardless again. He imagined that he had died with Marilys and was a ghost observing the living, wondering at their anxious rushing about, busy, busy, thinking of a million things but avoiding always the thought that one day they would die. What had Marilys thought when that wire tightened on her throat and the next world came rushing to meet her?

A bumper sticker told him that JESUS IS THE ANSWER. Leroy had no rival theory. Had Marilys met Jesus on the other side?

"Tell him that after I do what I have to do I'll be in touch."

He was talking to Marilys, something he had started to do on the drive north. It made him think they were not really separated, but closer than ever. After he had settled things with Gunther Kunz, he would join Marilys.

"I will be his instrument. Jesus will be punishing Gunther, not just me."

"Were you speaking to me?"

The little bitty lady who had sat next to him seemed to hope he had been addressing her.

"Do you believe in Jesus?"

"What an odd question."

"The reason I ask, a car just went by with JESUS IS THE ANSWER on its bumper."

The woman adopted an ambiguous expression, not knowing how Leroy intended this remark. "They're a lot of them around here, you know."

"Them?"

"The saved."

"How do they know?"

She nodded as if he had put his finger on the pertinent point. "Exactly. How do they know?"

"Maybe Jesus tells them."

"Maybe so."

"But you're not saved yourself?"

Considering the alternative, the woman was not quick to say no. "I'm Catholic."

"Aren't Catholics ever saved?"

"Only when we're dead." She said this with great firmness, and Leroy liked the answer. That Marilys was saved and safe with Jesus made sense, but how could anyone driving down the main street of Wyler know their future?

"What's going on over there?" Leroy pointed to the hotel. The deputy had just come out with his hand under Gunther's elbow, hurrying him along in an officious way. They went down the ramp of the garage and the sound of sirens was heard. A moment later two more sheriff's cruisers disappeared into the entrance of the garage.

"I wonder," said the little lady, sitting on the edge of the bench.

"Is there a lot of crime in this town?"

"In Wyler!" But her surprise gave way to another thought. "Where are you from?"

"Purgatory."

"Purgatory," she repeated with a frown. Her eyes darted toward him, then looked across the street.

"It's in Arizona. The next town is named Hell. Those settlers had odd senses of humor."

She was relieved. "Oh, look."

One of the cruisers had appeared. It hesitated on the edge of traffic and Leroy could see the fat deputy and Gunther in the backseat. The deputy at the wheel had the look of a man who wanted to hurry through what he was doing so he could go home and talk about it.

"They must have arrested him," Leroy said.

"I wonder what he did."

"From what I saw of him, he looks like the type that would do anything."

"Yes," she said with a little shiver. "Oh, here comes the bus."

It stopped, the door hissed open and the little lady boarded. She turned. "Aren't you getting on?"

"I have to get back to Purgatory."

At the courthouse Leroy bought a paper from a dispenser in the main lobby, studied the building directory, and then slowly mounted the spiral staircase under the great rotunda. There was a pewlike bench on the third floor, under the rotunda. Leroy sat and opened his paper.

He could see the furious Gunther being made to stand in front of a desk while a woman at a typewriter tapped out his answers to the questions she was putting to him. Only when the form was completed was Gunther permitted a call. Who did he know in Wyler?

The well-dressed, trim-figured man who emerged from the elevator fifteen minutes later looked familiar. A moment later he realized why. That was the face that had looked out confidently from the driver's license in Andrew Broom's wallet. The lawyer would be glad to know that the man who had stolen his car and wallet with all its contents was now in custody.

Thank God for this bench and the other one too, the one that the undertaker had provided at the bus stop. Arranging this unexplainable difficulty for Gunther would not be half so satisfying if he could not see the consequences of what he had done.

It was with the sense of a day's work well done that he got into the elevator and punched the *L* for lobby button. If just annoying Gunther Kunz was so satisfying, how glorious it would be to kill him.

TWENTY

Martha's idea to phone her client at the Hoosier and ask if he had been in touch with Andrew Broom, however patent a ruse, met with Susannah's approval.

"Why not? Then he'll know he's in good hands."

"Mine or Andrew's?"

Susannah patted both of Martha's hands, then led her across the room to Andrew's desk. What a command post it was! Looking out the windows of the office was a bit like coming in for a landing at the Wyler airport.

"Do you want me to dial it for you?"

Martha just gave Susannah a look. What a picture it created of Andrew Broom at work! Numbers dialed for him, errands run, messengers at his beck and call. It was all a little heady. Susannah read out the number and Martha dialed it.

"Gunther Kunz's room, please."

"One moment."

A ringing began in Martha's ear and went on and on until the desk broke in. "Mr. Kunz is not in his room."

"But that's not possible."

"Would you care to leave a message?"

"Thank you, no."

Susannah wore a quizzical frown. Martha turned away. She could not rid herself of the thought that once more something was going to prevent the sale of the Krueger place.

"He's not in his room."

"Maybe he's waiting for Andrew in the bar."

Of course. Martha's spirit rose immediately. She had to stop being such a Cassandra about the Krueger farm. Gunther wanted it, he was going to buy it; in a matter of days (with any kind of luck) the transaction would be as good as done.

Martha pushed back from the desk, thanked Susannah for the tea, said they simply had to get together soon, and headed for the door.

"The Krueger deal will bring us together. We must go to a movie some night."

"The three of us?"

"Andrew doesn't go to movies."

So Martha agreed that she and Susannah would see a movie soon. Driving past the Hoosier on her way home was not quite the direct route, but it was not outrageously a detour. All she meant to do was pass the building in which the first stage of the Krueger farm purchase was taking place. The parking space with twenty minutes left on the meter seemed a clear sign from God, so Martha pulled into it. The bar in the Hoosier was sufficiently well lit that a few times past the entrance convinced Martha that Andrew and her client were not there. In the lobby she picked up a phone and asked to speak to Gunther Kunz. She would just say what she might have said speaking from Andrew's desk.

"I'm sorry but Mr. Kunz is not in his room."

"Would you dial it?"

Martha could see the desk and she watched the young woman on the phone make a face and shrug at her male counterpart. What on earth was going on? Martha hung up and marched to the desk.

"What has happened to Gunther Kunz?"

The girl's eyes shifted as if she were about to lie.

"I am Mr. Kunz's secretary. Please ring his room."

She was asked to come around the desk. In a small room behind it the girl told her.

"The sheriff came and arrested him. I don't know why. But you have a right to know and . . ."

Martha Doremus would have categorically denied that she had ever fainted. She slumped to the floor at the girl's words and some moments later found herself sitting upright, the little room full, a glass of water being thrust into her face.

She had never been so embarrassed in her life. All those concerned, attentive faces looking down on her as if she were impossibly fragile, as if she were old. Martha got to her feet, but she needed support. She sat down again.

Someone asked if the lady was staying in the hotel. This reduced Martha to the status of a stranger in the town where she had lived all her life.

"I live at 2158 Blumenfeld," she said through clenched teeth.

"Is that where you want to go?"

"That is where I live."

It was a measure of her discombobulation that she allowed a taxi to be called for her. She sat in stoic silence, still surrounded by a remote professional concern, until the taxi came. She was convoyed through the lobby and outside before she remembered that her car was parked just down the street. To mention that now might suggest that she had lost the ability to manage her own life. So she was swept away in a taxi with a diminished escort waving her off. She kept her eyes straight ahead when the cab went by her parked car.

Safely within her own house, Martha burst into tears. For five minutes she cried all but uncontrollably. Then she carefully poured an ounce of sweet sherry and sipped it, trusting in its restorative powers. She sat in the living room as evening fell. She would take the bus downtown and pick up her car, but later, not yet.

She was seventy-three years old. Her health was good. Her mind—despite the embarrassment in the Hoosier Towers—was sound. At least she thought it was sound. Did a time come when one knew that the sharp edge was gone, forgetfulness frequent, control going? To frame the question was to know the answer. For the first time, Martha Doremus had a sense of what lay ahead for her.

She did not like to think of the future. It was not simply that the past was more attractive. It was no longer possible to project ahead a year, three years, five, ten, in the untroubled confidence that she would still be alive. She could die today. Fainting as she had could be a first symptom. Who knew what was going on in the human brain? Martha had watched a program on public television devoted to brain research and brain surgery. The brain looked like molded jello, fat, some unshelled creature from the deep. Eventually, it would let her down. She feared far more the betrayal of her brain than of her heart.

The room was in twilight when she picked up the phone to call the sheriff. Of course, she did not know the number. She dialed the operator and asked for assistance. Her voice sounded so weak and vulnerable that the operator dialed the number for her.

When the ringing sounded in her ear, she sat erect, closed her eyes, and determined to be her normal self.

"County sheriff."

"This is Martha Doremus. Would you please ask Mr. Andrew Broom to come to the phone."

"Broom? This is the sheriff's office."

"Mr. Broom is an attorney who is there speaking with Mr. Gunther Kunz."

"Just a minute."

Martha tapped time with the toe of her shoe as she waited. Her normal voice had restored her to order as well as galvanized the one who had answered the phone.

"Ma'am?"

140

"Yes."

"Gunther Kunz has been released from custody. Him and his lawyer left."

Him and his lawyer? Ye gods. "Thank you."

She opened her eyes as she returned the phone to its cradle. Now then. She must go downtown for her car. While she was there, she could see her client at his hotel. Her jaw worked as she exorcised humiliating memories of the lobby of the Hoosier. She had heard that pilots who survive an accident are sent up into the air as soon as possible. It was important not to let failure assume the proportions of a permanent condition. But she would call the hotel now and see if he had returned.

"Mr. Kunz's room, please." She had actually tried to disguise her voice.

"He doesn't answer, ma'am," she was told in a minute and a half.

"Has he returned to the hotel?"

"His key is here."

"Thank you."

Martha clicked the phone twice and dialed Susannah Broom.

"Martha, have you heard?"

"Tell me."

"The man who wants the Krueger farm was arrested. They thought he was the man who killed a girl in Indianapolis. Oh, it's the most complicated story. Anyway, Andrew seems to have gotten it all straightened out. Kunz is here now."

"I tried to reach him at his hotel and he wasn't there."

141

"Well, now you know why."

"Yes."

"I couldn't persuade you to join us, could I, Martha? I'm just tossing together pasta and a salad."

"Susannah, I would love to. But I'll have to ask for a rain check."

Her composure somewhat restored, Martha took the bus downtown, where she found a parking ticket on her car. The sheriff had gotten to her before she got to the sheriff.

TWENTY-ONE

"I must say you've taken this very well," Andrew Broom said to Gunther. "It's an incredible confusion."

Gunther shook his head tolerantly. "Obviously someone was diverting attention from themselves."

"To you."

Gunther's teeth were gray in color and when he laughed, tipping his head back, extensive dental work was put on display. "It could have been anyone, I suspect. Why your credit cards and wallet, for that matter?"

"They were stolen."

"Well."

Maybe it could have happened to anyone; Andrew wasn't sure. He couldn't make up his mind about Gunther Kunz. That the man was his client was undeniable, but a real-estate transaction is a minimal kind of representation. And Kunz seemed to block certain lines of conversation. In any case, the title search that had been made for the Krueger property satisfied Andrew that the purchaser faced no liens or claims.

"How much did Mrs. Doremus tell you of the Krueger property?"

"The extent of it? I walked it a bit and think I got a good sense of the place. The house seems in very good repair."

"It hasn't really been occupied much in recent times. Less than a year ago a man named Palmer restored it. The land was always farmed, rented to neighbors."

"Neighbors." Gunther smiled. "It sounds strange to me that people who live so far away should be called neighbors."

"You've lived in the city all your life?"

"Cities. Here and abroad."

"And now you want to retire to rural solitude?"

"You make it sound like an unrealistic, romantic dream."

"No. But one place is like another in most respects. Why did you choose Wyler?"

"If I may say so, Broom, you do not match any preconception I had of the small-town lawyer. Obviously, living here is a matter of choice with you."

"Yes. But it's also my hometown."

"I envy you those roots."

Roots? Is that what they were? Andrew supposed they could be called that, but somehow the image of himself as a mythic chthonic creature not wholly emerged from earth seemed a more romantic dream than any Gunther Kunz might indulge.

"The previous owner, Palmer, is dead."

"I gathered that from Mrs. Doremus."

"He was murdered. Shot down in the backyard."

Gunther shook his head. "These are violent times. I don't imagine I can wholly escape that fact by moving here. Who shot him?"

"The sheriff thought you did. That's why you were arrested."

"You mean they think the man they thought I was did it?"

"Yes."

Gunther leaned forward, holding his glass of beer in both hands. He had wanted nothing but beer since coming to the house, beer before the meal, beer during the meal, beer now as they sat on the sun porch in the cool of the evening. Susannah had left them alone, but the sounds from the kitchen indicated her presence. "The monkey business with my car means that Leroy White is in Wyler, doesn't it?"

"I would think so."

"He certainly put me through my paces."

"It could have been anyone."

Gunther looked at him over the rim of his glass as he drained its contents. Andrew was merely repeating what Gunther had suggested earlier. That Leroy had wanted to divert attention from himself rather than onto Gunther.

But Andrew couldn't keep back the curious thought: What if the choice of Gunther had been deliberate?

145

"I'm interested in the history of the place. Is there a local historical association?"

Andrew mentioned the WHA, located in an old firehouse on Tarkington, just outside the downtown area.

"Earl Sanders is the curator." Andrew hesitated. "Something of an eccentric. But he's gathered together an impressive collection of memorabilia."

"What about the library?"

"You could look there too. The *Dealer* has been publishing since 1878. Their archivist is knowledgeable." It seemed a safe word. If Earl Sanders was eccentric, what was Bernice Beresford?

"A house that age must have quite a history of its own."

"Perhaps not, if history means written accounts. Memories die with those who have them. I'm only in my mid-forties, and already there are aspects of Wyler as it was when I was a boy that exist nowhere but in a few very mortal brains. The previous generation is all but gone and they took to the grave memories that can never be recovered."

"Krueger," Gunther said. "Any Kruegers still around? I wouldn't want to feel that I was usurping anyone's ancestral home."

"When the Kruegers left, they left as a family. One day they lived here; the next day they were all gone."

"Why?"

"You must remember the Second World War."

"Of course."

"The Kruegers were German. Germany was the

enemy. Old Krueger took it pretty badly. I gather the family had been through it before, in World War I."

"But where could they go?"

"The theory was that they changed their name and began over. There are no Kruegers in Wyler and it might be difficult to find any anywhere, at least ones connected with our Kruegers."

"Surely they didn't just abandon the farm?"

"No."

"They sold it first?"

"They tried to."

When Andrew took Gunther back to the hotel, there was a heavyset man of indeterminate age lounging on the bench at the bus stop; he looked familiar, though Andrew could not imagine why. Some realist painting of the thirties? Perhaps. When he pulled out into the street again, the bench was empty. Had a bus come and gone?

But his mind returned to the thought that had come to him talking with Gunther: that what had happened to Palmer might be explained by the past of the house rather than Palmer's past in New York.

But it was another, more particular thought that intrigued him most. When the Kruegers left Wyler, however sudden the decision had been, they had left their property to be sold by Emil Doremus. The realtor had to know how to reach them. Although he had not sold the house, he had rented the land; the income had to go somewhere. For that matter, to whom would Martha pay the income from the sale of the house?

★

Later, lying in the dark beside Susannah, he re-
marked that Gunther was an enigmatic man.

"He has ice in his veins."

"But he's always smiling."

"Maybe he has gas in his tummy."

He put his hand on hers and pressed gently. "You
don't like him."

"If he asked me to run away with him, I wouldn't
even be tempted."

"You'd better not be."

"Did you tell him about the house? About Palmer?"

"Martha must have told him."

"Oh, I don't think so, Andrew."

"Well, he wasn't really surprised when I told
him Palmer had been shot in the backyard of the
place."

"The sheriff! They must have told him what they
thought Leroy White had done. They thought he was
Leroy, didn't they?"

"Once they proved he wasn't Andrew Broom."

Susannah dug him in the ribs.

"Do you know what I think Susannah?"

"Not always." She rolled on her side and pressed
against him.

"The Doremuses must have been dealing with the
Kruegers all along. Sending them rental money, acting as agent for them."

"So?"

"So they had to know where they were."

"Why does that matter? Is someone looking for them?"

Andrew adjusted his arm so that her head leaned against his own. "Gunther is interested in the history of the property, and of the family."

"Martha won't be able to help him there."

"Why not?"

"Her husband bought the property, Andrew. Getting rid of it is not something she's doing for someone else."

He nodded. He had learned that during the Palmer transaction, and had promptly forgotten it. What he had not learned was exactly when Emil Doremus had bought the farm from Krueger. It had to have been some time after the Kruegers left, which meant that Emil would have known where they were for at least a little while after they left Wyler.

"Gimme a kiss."

"Kiss you! I shouldn't even be in bed with you."

Two hours later Andrew got up to warm some milk and try to coax sleep. His mind was a riot of thoughts in search of a theme, and he desperately wanted to get some sleep—if only as a relief from pestering speculation. As he passed through the living room, he heard a sound outside, carried with eerie distinctness at this time of night. The sound of footsteps. Slow, almost sauntering, footsteps. Andrew stood at the front window, the slats of the blinds laying strips of moonlight on his pajamaed body.

The man going by on the walk across the street looked to be the same fellow he had noticed sitting on the bus-stop bench across from the Hoosier. And

149

then he knew why the man was familiar. He had been sitting on a bench in the courthouse when Andrew came out of the elevator to intercede for Gunther Kunz with the sheriff.

Was he being watched? It was difficult not to think so. Andrew moved to a dining-room window so that he could continue to see the man. Heavy, his feet moving in a kind of duck-walk, the fellow's manner suggested that this was midday and there was nothing odd at all about his strolling down the street.

TWENTY-TWO

The poncholike vestment Bernice Beresford wore—in equivocal tribute to the one–sixty-fourth Miami Indian blood that coursed through the veins that doubtless existed beneath a comfortable cushion of flesh—was embroidered with symbols that she was more than willing to have interpreted for her.

"That looks like a swastika," the man said, pointing to a symbol that occurred at intervals of three in the string of symbols bordering the garment.

"I'll take your word for that," Bernice said. She laid a gray braid carefully over her right shoulder.

"But that's what it is."

"Do you want to know something?"

"Sure."

"I don't know what a swastika is."

He stepped back. "Of course you wouldn't. You're not nearly old enough."

Bernice decided he was cute. The man had to be her own age or less.

"You're just passing through?"

"Maybe not."

Well, well. "So what can I do you for?"

"Do you know of the Krueger farm?"

Bernice put her folded arms on the counter and looked up at him with eyes she hoped were not too awfully bloodshot. "Can Pavarotti sing?"

His smile was puzzled.

"It's my job. I know Wyler like the back of my hand."

She held out her hand and he took it in his and began to examine it. Her smile had become playful.

"Where is the Krueger farm?"

She came around the counter without freeing her hand from his. The movement suggested another and she turned gracefully despite her weight beneath their joined hands.

"Do you Lindy?" she asked over her shoulder.

"Was that dance named for Lindbergh?"

"Let's look it up." And she pulled him toward her computer.

They looked up the Lindy, they looked up the swastika, and eventually they looked up Krueger in the back files of the *Dealer*. That this was possible was due to Bernice's insistent nagging over a period of two years. No one could believe that she was that sold on computers. Her visitor couldn't.

"You don't look the computer type."

"Just calculating?"

"You know what I mean."

"I do! Normally, I can't find my toes with both eyes open."

She fluttered her eyes as she said this. Since the age of nine (when she had begun to develop) Bernice had taken pride in her breasts. Even in Big Girl shops, clerks were astounded by her dimensions. Unfortunately, she now measured about the same around the middle as she did around the hips and bust, but she had learned that men are not as much in thrall to the aesthetic ideal as is generally believed.

Actually, it had been a computer programmer involved in the public library project who had turned Bernice's head in the matter of the electronic revolution in information retrieval. He had talked that way, and it was easy to imagine it as a coded obscene language expressing his uncontrollable desire for her body. That had been in the picture, as events proved, but he was dead serious about the computer jargon. Bernice could sit for hours, chins in her hand, and listen to him talk about input.

"Isn't that what golfers do?"

Wayne ignored it. He was on subdirectories now. Almost to Bernice's surprise, she came to understand what he was talking about. One night, after hours, she showed him her archives at the *Dealer*. He couldn't believe the system that had been developed over the years.

"This should all be computerized."

"How would you go about doing that if you were to do it, Wayne?"

"It's largely a matter of input."

"I knew it."

"I'd develop the program, then hire half a dozen operators to enter the contents of the paper."

So Bernice had begun her campaign; she thought of it as a way to keep Wayne in town. He was fun and all that, and it would have been nice if he spent another half-year or so in Wyler—but the powers that be were not interested.

Even when Wayne finished and left town (after a very sentimental farewell celebration), the idea of computerizing the newspaper archives stayed with Bernice. Finally, thanks to sheer persistence, she won the day. They sent a girl to devise the program, a meatless little thing who chewed on her hair and was smart as a whip.

"Can you print that out?" Gunther asked.

"Can Pavarotti sing."

"I'd like copies."

"Ten cents a page."

"Go ahead."

"Ten cents a dance." She was singing. Gunther—she was already calling him Gunther—stood very close beside her, but how could he avoid it, as her enemies might say. They printed out for hours.

By then she knew he intended to buy the Krueger place and all this was to get a sense of its history.

"The house is haunted, you know."

"Because of the murder?"

"Oh, it goes way back. To when I was a girl." She gave him a bump with her hip.

"Do you believe in ghosts?"

"I'm not dumb enough to say I don't."

"Did you know the Kruegers?"

"I'm not old enough to know what a swastika is and you ask if I knew the Kruegers."

"Why do you say that?" His eyes were suddenly ice-cold and Bernice felt uneasy alone with him there in the *Wyler Dealer* archives.

"It was your joke."

She explained it to him, for God's sake, and his eyes became warm again. Whew. What a guy. He was built nicely though, she had to give him that, and he was responsive enough when she kept close.

"I am starved," she announced, looking at the massive Timex dwarfed by her wrist. It was close enough to noon to beat it.

"I never eat lunch."

"Good idea. What do you do, drink it?"

He moved out of range of her elbow. "I don't eat lunch, but I understand that most people do. Bernice, I want to thank you for all your valuable time."

"Come on back."

"I think I may."

"I think I may, I think I might." She was singing again. "Do you know it?"

He shook his head.

"I want an invitation to the Krueger place when you buy it."

"I'm thinking of having a Halloween party."

It was a joke. He ought to warn a person first. She promised to come as Casper's aunt. He didn't know who Casper was.

"Where've you been all your life, drawing swastikas on walls?"

His eyes went cold again. Geez. She wasn't sorry

to see him go. She might not even go to his Halloween party. That would show him.

The fat guy came in before she could close up and
leave.

"I was just going to lunch."

"Where do you go?"

She looked him over. She didn't like fat people.
She felt fatter with someone her own size. But this
guy had a bald head and moon face and very gentle
eyes.

"Do you know Il Giardino?"

"I don't even know the well one."

Bernice threw her arm around him and hugged.
"You can have lunch with me any day."

They were still serving in the courtyard of Il
Giardino, which was covered with grapevines that
were now heavy with fruit; a little sun got through
though, making it tolerable enough. They were given
a table under a great cluster of grapes.

"This place makes me feel like *Quo Vadis*."

She stood and freed several grapes, sat and, leaning across the table, put one in his mouth, mushing
it a bit to stain his lips.

"How'd you like to be Peter Ustinov?"

"What's your role?"

"Danish."

The two of them roared under the grapevine. Thank
God she had ditched Gunther. She told King—his
name was Leroy, which means king, something he
claimed not to have known—about Gunther and his
lack of sense of humor and what a godsend King was.

"What does Gunther mean?"

"It's classified."

"What did he want?"

"He's buying the Krueger place. Do you know it?" He nodded. "He wanted everything there had ever been in the paper about the family and farm."

"He's buying the place?"

"I know, I know. I told him it was haunted."

"Was there much information on the farm?"

"On the family. I was surprised. They haven't lived here for forty years, so I had to go back a ways."

"I suppose he was more interested in the last forty years."

"Oh no. It was only Kruegers he wanted to find out about. Know what that is?" She pointed to her poncho.

"A swastika?"

"Everybody knows but me. He told me that's what it was."

"Was Krueger a Nazi or something?"

"What a memory. You know, I had forgotten all about the way they were teased. Maybe people were ashamed. One of the Krueger girls, Celette, was in my room and the boys used to march behind her the way the German army did."

"Goosestep."

"Sometimes. Kids are crazy."

"And then they become adults."

TWENTY-THREE

A brass pole rose from the first floor up through Earl
Sanders's office on the second floor, but it was inad-
visable to ask him if that was the way he got down-
stairs. Earl could not abide levity (as a general
rule), but when it was directed against the Wyler
Historical Association and his stewardship of it,
watch out. In the first place, the collection of historical
materials gathered together in the former firehouse
was impressive. Experts had told him this. In the
second place, Earl could lay claim to the title of
expert himself, at least in Wyler.

When he went off to Bloomington after high school,
his intention had been to prepare himself for a degree in
library science. His high-school counselor had said
Earl was a natural librarian. The counselor was as-
sistant basketball coach and shook his head sadly

when he said it, but Earl had recognized the truth of the observation immediately. He was precise and neat and inclined to be pedantic. He wore bow ties and nothing but bow ties from the age of nineteen. It was his trademark. He wore them because they permitted the immaculate expanse of his shirt front to show. Ordinary ties too often concealed soiled linen—that was Earl's view of the matter.

But if he had intended to marry library science, he had been seduced by history. He did take quite a number of courses of bibliography and archival procedures, but he loved history with an almost illicit passion. Unfortunately, he was only a consumer of the research of others and did not himself have the knack of pushing forward the frontiers of our knowledge of the past. A university career was closed to him. He had given the odd course at IUSB, the branch of the state university located in South Bend, but he did not have the credentials for a permanent appointment. Teach high school? He would have preferred the Foreign Legion. He had been saved, there was no other word for it, by the last will and testament of Moses and Miriam Kaplan. Kaplan's was a store specializing in work clothes—high quality, low prices. The Kaplans had no children, and they had not belonged to the synagogue. They left their money to the city for the express purpose of founding a historical society. Along with their money they bequeathed the business records of Kaplan Klothes.

Earl Sanders applied for and got the job. He had been in on the planning, the development, and the ongoing operation of the WHA. In a sense, Earl

Sanders was the WHA. For eleven years he had been molding and shaping the historical society, using the building he had been given for the purpose so adeptly that it was his hope that no one even thought of it as a firehouse anymore. Thin sandy hair that lifted from his head at the slightest breeze and was constantly charged with static electricity, large lensed rimless glasses, the bow tie—he looked as he had at nineteen and as he would look at fifty-nine, not young or old or in-between.

The zeal with which he had solicited records and papers and family Bibles and old stereopticons, anything and everything that told some part of the history of the region, was the hallmark of his regime. He wanted the citizens to think of their letters and papers and records as ultimately destined for the WHA.

"You'll run out of space," Grimes, his old professor, warned. Grimes was one of the experts who pronounced the WHA extraordinary.

Earl only smiled. He had no fear on that score.

"You'll microfilm?" Grimes asked.

"A little. The trick, as I see it, is having everything entered and accounted for on the computer. It is less important where it physically is than that it can be immediately located."

"Ah," said Grimes.

Gorman, another professor, and another expert who praised Earl's work, urged his protégé to use the computer to the hilt. "It's the wave of the future, Earl. It's the only way to handle the past."

Thus it was that when a man calling himself Gunther Kunz came in one September morn and asked what Earl had on the Krueger family who had owned a farm on Route 16, all Earl had to do was put the question to his computer.

"Can you see the screen, Mr. Kunz? There isn't much, but there's a little. Some of these entries refer to papers at the courthouse and elsewhere. Eventually, they will come here so I've been anticipating that by putting them on the computer now."

Gunther came around the desk and leaned over Earl's shoulder.

"Yes," he said. "Those papers I know of. Any personal stuff?"

Earl hit a digit and entered it. Three items appeared: the grades the Krueger children had received in school; a newspaper account of a church supper at which Grandfather Krueger described first settling here; Emil Doremus.

"Emil Doremus?"

"Real-estate matters, correspondence, payments of rent to Krueger."

"You have that here?" Gunther rubbed his bald head as if for luck.

"Not in this building, no. You'll notice that the descriptions of what we have are quite uninformative. This is a preliminary entry. In time, I will go through the material and enter more detailed information."

Earl would have been perfectly willing to tell his visitor more, a good deal more, about the WHA, but the man seemed satisfied with what he had seen on the screen. Did he want Earl to have the materials sent over from the city's warehouse? Effusive thanks, but no thanks.

161

Oh, Earl was used to this limited interest on the part of others in what was his own life's work. One had to be careful not to be overly informative. Most people have a limited ability to absorb data. About the only one he could count on having an interest equal to his own was Bernice Beresford. He sighed and rolled his eyes to the ceiling. Dear Bernice. She was so fat and breathy and she insisted on rubbing against one as if she were in heat. That he had overcome his aversion for her person said how much he needed someone with whom to discuss archival matters.

Speak of the devil, or at least think of her. Bernice called that same day, and they agreed to meet for dinner.

"Has the about-to-be new owner of the Krueger farm been to see you?"

"Is that what it was all about? He didn't mention he was buying the place. But I showed him what I have."

"So did I." There was a suggestive lilt in her voice. Honestly, the woman was so horny. But when he chided her, she insisted it was all talk.

"Is that what is meant by oral sex?"

Her laugh boomed through the restaurant where they were dining. Earl felt like pulling his napkin over his head and escaping. Obviously, it would not do now to let her know that his question had been asked in all sincerity.

"He didn't seem new to town at all."

"Earl, how would you know? Nothing interests you until it has collected all kinds of dust."

"*Et tu, Brute?*"

"Speak English, dammit, or it's so long, Oo Long."

"People in the same trade should be natural friends."

"Are you suggesting one of us is unnatural."

Earl closed his eyes. He lived a life as pure as an angel, and always had; yet, from high school on, people had made these suggestive remarks about what is somewhat bewilderingly now called one's sexual orientation. Of course, he didn't like girls, but he liked boys no better. He had explained to Bernice that he was a misanthrope.

"Miss what?"

"Oh, shut up."

"You brought it up."

Earl exhaled as if to expel that topic. "I like the way he rubs his bald head for luck."

"Who?"

"Gunther Kunz."

"He's not bald."

"Not bald? He doesn't have a hair atop his head."

Bernice stared. "Then he was wearing a toupee when he came here. But he couldn't have been. I couldn't have been fooled. It was real hair."

"He was there yesterday?"

"Yesterday morning."

"Well, all his hair has fallen out since then, Bernice. But he didn't lose any weight."

"How heavy was he?"

Earl put it as carefully as he could. "I wouldn't call him heavy. He's no heavier than you are."

"You know who that was that came to see you, Earl?"

163

"I think I do, yes."

"Well, you don't. The man who came to see you is Leroy White. He came to see me too."

"Bernice, he quite distinctly said he was Gunther Kunz."

"I don't care. He wasn't. The man you describe is Leroy White."

"Then tell me why both of them are asking questions about the Kruegers?"

"I can't. Leroy didn't ask me any such questions at all."

"Then why did he come see you?"

A longish pause. "Good question."

★

How odd. Earl didn't like it. He liked it a lot less when he went to the city's warehouse and found that the box containing the Krueger material was missing.

TWENTY-FOUR

When Martha looked out and saw Andrew Broom coming toward the house, her feelings were mixed. The previous day's nightmare was once more vividly before her, and her face grew hot with embarrassment. On the other hand, the sight of him was reassuring. In any case, she had no intention of letting him see how shaken she had been by the fear that the sale of the Krueger farm to Gunther Kunz would not go through. She opened the door wide and stood in it, wearing her most welcoming smile.

"I understand my prospective purchaser was arrested."

Andrew laughed deprecatingly, bent to kiss her cheek, and came inside. "I got him unarrested again, so don't worry about it."

165

"What was it all about?"

"My lips are sealed until I'm given a cup of tea."

Martha enjoyed having someone to fuss over. He came with her into the kitchen, and leaned against a counter. His easy manner was contagious.

"They actually thought he was a murderer?"

"They were meant to think that. Someone went to a good deal of trouble to make them think that Gunther Kunz was Leroy White."

"Who would do that?"

"Now, Martha, I can understand the sheriff and his merry men being confused about that, but not you. Who is the obvious candidate for wanting Gunther arrested as Leroy?"

"Leroy?"

"Of course."

"Do you mean the man who killed Willard Palmer is in town?"

It was obvious that Andrew had no intention of frightening her, but she could hardly take lightly the suggestion that a man who had shot Willard Palmer from hiding, and later brutally murdered his young girl companion was wandering around Wyler.

"Well, wandering around the garage of the Hoosier Towers, anyway." But Andrew's eyes drifted to the window as if he were thinking of something else.

"Do you suppose he really expected the police to think Gunther Kunz was a mad-dog killer?"

"I see you read the *Dealer*."

She did indeed, religiously. Her business kept her aware of what was going on in the city only to a degree. As for the buying and selling of real estate, the disposition of properties, rumors about developers and government money, all that came her way as a matter of course. But reading the *Dealer* was like getting news of some strange far-off place, the kind of place where she would not care to live. It took an exercise of the imagination to put the Wyler of the *Dealer* together with her own daily doings in the town. But then her Wyler was a complicated mixture of the present and all that had been. Who but a long-established realtor would continue to call a property the Krueger farm when the last Krueger had left the region decades ago?

Martha clapped her hand over her mouth and stared at Andrew.

"What is it, Martha?"

"I've just had a dreadful idea."

"Tell me."

"But it's wholly fanciful."

They had their tea right there at the kitchen table and it was the easiest thing in the world to go on babbling to Andrew Broom.

"Imagine one of the Kruegers coming back, Andrew, and resenting the present occupant of the house they had left so stealthily. People do, you know. I see it all the time. The young couple who bought the Beeson house on Portage told me they were visited almost weekly by one Beeson or another who had been raised in the house. Nor were they reluctant to comment negatively on the changes the Werners are making. They act as if the property is still theirs and the new

167

owner is a kind of invader. It happens often. So just imagine . . ."

"The last Krueger," he offered, smiling.

"I said it was fanciful."

"Martha, it's as good as any other theory they have."

"He shoots Willard and then tries to scare Gunther off before he can buy the property."

"Meanwhile killing a girl in Indianapolis? Martha, fear not. Nothing will interfere with the sale of the farm."

"If only I had that in writing."

"What you want in writing is the sale."

It was good to feel that Andrew was on her side— and she did feel it, despite the document he had written on Willard Palmer's behalf. As far as Andrew could see, what he had to do for Kunz had already been done in the main for Willard, and there was no need to duplicate the title search.

"I *would* like you to refresh my mind on a few things."

"Of course."

"You described the Kruegers as leaving town stealthily. My vague memory is that they were spoken of as if they had fled."

"Old Krueger had been given a bad time during the First War and with the coming of the Second he became fearful that German-Americans were going to be treated as the enemy. I don't know if he had any objective basis for that . . . No, I can't say that. He did have reasons. You and I might say they were not very good reasons, but I wonder if we're able to judge."

"But he came to Emil before leaving?"

"He put the property up for sale."

"With Emil?"

"Believe me, in the circumstances, Emil was not optimistic. In the early forties, there was suddenly money again, but buying a farm was not that attractive. The movement was in the other direction."

"Where did Emil get in touch with Krueger?"

"We never saw him again, Andrew."

"So it was only through correspondence."

"That's right."

"What was Krueger's address?"

"Oh, I don't remember."

"Would there be correspondence?"

"Emil kept very careful records. As I do."

Andrew sat back and sipped his tea meditatively. Without prelude, the name Franklin Meecham formed in Martha's mind and it was all she could do not to cry out. Whatever the association was—Andrew a lawyer, Meecham allegedly a lawyer from Baltimore—those two phone calls came back to her.

"What is it, Martha?"

"It's probably nothing."

"That means you think it's something."

She told him. Meecham had a buyer who would make Palmer an offer he could not resist for the old Krueger farm.

"Is that how he referred to it, the Krueger farm?"

"I'm almost sure."

169

"Then what?"

"He called back and I lied. I said I had broached the matter with Willard Palmer and he had dismissed the idea of leaving the house he was still settling into. That was the end of it."

Andrew thought about it. "An offer Palmer couldn't resist?"

"That's what he said."

"He certainly gave up easily, didn't he? How do people act when they set their minds on buying a house?"

Martha smiled. "Emil always said that every house is for sale. They don't have to be listed. If someone really wants a house, there is a good chance they can interest the owner in selling it. There are exceptions."

"But wouldn't they give up the idea only with difficulty?"

"Oh yes."

"Then why did Meecham subside without pursuing the matter?"

"Well, he was representing someone else."

She poured them each another cup of tea. Was he thinking what she was, that her fanciful talk of the last Krueger returning to avenge his family had been prompted by the suppressed memory of Meecham's phone call? This is how she put it to Andrew, who reacted with surprise.

"Where did you pick up all this psychological jargon?"

No need to be diverted into admitting that she was an avid reader of pop psychology. She had begun in the hope that it would be a business aid, knowing what makes people tick, but she had become an addict. Honestly, some of it brought a blush to the cheek. There seemed to be no subjects that could not be discussed.

"Andrew, I checked on Meecham and he does not practice law in Baltimore. The phone calls were phony."

It just came out. They both laughed, which helped a bit, but Martha was sure that her earlier imaginings were far more than that. It was the man who had called himself Franklin Meecham who was in town, who had shot Willard Palmer and was harassing Gunther Kunz.

"Then we know what he looks like, Martha. He is fat and bald and middle-aged."

"We must tell the sheriff!"

"The description I just gave you comes from the sheriff." He made a dismissing gesture. "Can I see that correspondence between Emil and Krueger?"

"Well, it's all right with me, but you'll have to go to the Wyler Historical Association. Earl Sanders talked me into donating early business correspondence to the archives there."

"Do you mean anyone can go into that place and read your letters?"

"That was my objection. No. They are under what Earl calls an embargo until the turn of the century. In the meantime, no one can see them without my permission."

"Would you call and tell him I want to come down and see those letters?"

But Earl did not answer and Louis, the high-school boy Earl called his apprentice, took the message. Mr. Andrew Broom would be dropping by to check on some papers she had donated to the WHA and it was all right with her that he be allowed to see them.

"Will you tell Mr. Sanders that?"

"As soon as he gets back from the warehouse," Louis said in his high, careful voice.

TWENTY-FIVE

When he left the courthouse with Andrew Broom, breathing free air again after having been certain that, however fantastic the reason for his arrest, even these provincial police would somehow stumble on his real crime, he did not want to go back to the Hoosier Towers. Equally, he did not want to tell the lawyer of his reluctance. So he had hopped out of the car, gone through the revolving door into the lobby, and angled toward the door leading onto a side street. He went to the corner and waited until the bus stopped across the street, sprinting for it and getting aboard despite some jackass who had been lolling on a bench and decided at the last minute to get on the bus. Gunther's rear end was nearly caught in the door as the driver pulled away from the curb.

He sat immediately behind the driver, which gave him a good view through the windshield. His destination? He did not know. He had the clothes he wore, less than a hundred dollars in cash, and his credit cards. He was going to go underground and, as he thought of it, was more than prepared to do so. From this moment, no one was going to know where Gunther Kunz was. He would leave no trail that could be followed.

The sight of a bike rack at a shopping center gave him the inspiration he had been waiting for. He left the bus by the front door, ignoring the driver's protests, and swam in the sea of the people for a time, going past the parked bicycles once, twice, seeing that there was one ten-speed that was not chained in place. But when he came back to take it, a gangly youth with red and yellow hair was wheeling it out of the rack. Was the boy the owner or a fellow thief?

All the other bikes were chained and locked. Gunther went into a hardware store and walked aimlessly up and down the aisles. He did not want to take a taxi because then it would be known where he had gone. Another bus? But his eye caught a gun section and he drifted toward it, checking it out as he advanced. Shotguns and .22's only, of course, but a .22 would be good enough.

He leaned against the counter, head thrust forward, squinting at the guns on display.

"Can I help you, sir?" The clerk was in his forties, with short, thin hair brushed forward on his head in a pathetic effort to conceal his baldness.

"I didn't know a person could just come in here and buy a gun."

The clerk looked at him through narrowed eyes. "What's your point, sir? It's perfectly legal. Some people only like the laws they agree with, of course ..."

"No, no, no. Don't get me wrong. I've been wanting a gun for some time. I'm being driven crazy by raccoons and I think there's only one solution to the problem."

The clerk's manner changed. He said confidentially, "Be careful if you live in town."

"Oh, I'm a very good shot. I was a sharpshooter in the army." Gunther could have bitten his tongue. What a time to brag. He was trying to be anonymous, not assert any singularity. "Let me see a .22."

"Yours sounds like a shotgun problem to me."

"Maybe. But I'd like to see that gun there."

The clerk carried the rifle to him and chattered away while Gunther checked it out. He tried to do this without drawing attention to how well he knew guns. The .22 was worth what was being asked for it and nothing more. Thoughts of the M1 teased him and he wished he still had it. But this .22 would suffice.

When he left the hardware store, he had the rifle in its box and two boxes of shells in a plastic bag. He felt better than he had in weeks. At the curb was a stubby little bus and a line of elderly people slowly climbing into it. SUNSET VILLAGE was printed in large black letters on its lemon yellow side. Gunther joined the line and sat in a backseat next to a deaf

man whose ears were blocked by large plastic de-
vices that seemed no help at all. He shouted all the
way to the retirement home about events that had
apparently taken place a quarter of a century ago.
From time to time, he rolled a rheumy eye to Gunther,
who nodded in commiseration. There was a queru-
lous tone to all the raised voices in the little bus,
multiple indictments of the world. No one seemed to
notice or care about the rock music that assaulted
the ear, the choice of the young driver. If they noticed that Gunther was a comparative youngster,
they gave no indication of it. Self-absorption charac-
terized them all. They did not carry on conversations
so much as harangue the world in one another's
presence.

Sunset Village was a collection of low buildings
with exaggerated eaves making them seem lower
yet. Gunther wondered if one had to stoop to enter
them. He got off the bus and wandered away as the
others did. He was on the south side of Wyler, and
it was evening; he did not know where he would
sleep that night, only that it would not be in Sunset
Village. He nearly walked into a three-wheeled bike
with a large wire basket. He put his purchases in the
basket and got on the trike and began to move slowly
away. No shout, no protest was directed at him, and
he wheeled out of the entrance as an itinerary formed
in his mine. He knew where he was. He knew where
he was going.

It was impossible to make good time on the three-
wheeler, but he pedaled parallel to the river until he

came upon a good north-south road. Heavily traveled. He kept to the berm but rode to the accompaniment of warning horns as traffic whooshed past a few feet to his left. Unnerving at first, he took comfort from it because it promised a bridge over the river. And eventually he came to a bridge, but a bridge without provision for pedestrians, let alone three-wheeled bikes. A three-wheeled bicycle, it occurred to him, was self-contradictory.

Gunther got off the trike and wheeled it down into the ditch and through, and then got in front of it to slow its descent to the river. A hundred witnesses to the deed, but what could he do? He left the trike beneath the bridge. Then he started along the river in the direction of the trestle.

It was his first chance to reflect on that sonofabitch Leroy, and Gunther saw that the dumbest thing he had ever done was to leave Leroy alive in Indianapolis. It would have made more sense to get rid of him than the girl, far more sense, if he was going to do only one of them. He should have taken care of them both then. Now he had no choice. He had to get to Leroy before Leroy got to him.

What had been the point of that business with the car? Obviously, Leroy had come north to avenge his girl. Gunther did not like to think that if Leroy had done all that funny business to make the police think he was Leroy, it would have been easy for him to kill Gunther in the garage.

Why hadn't he? The switching of plates and the planting of Andrew Broom's wallet, all that, was an

177

elaborate way of letting Gunther know that Leroy was in town. Or had he thought that once the police had him in custody they would find out about Willard Palmer? More likely he wanted his girl avenged. But it was most likely that he was just playing games and Gunther didn't like that one damned bit.

Not when the game was being played on him, that is. Now he would be the hunter again and Leroy the hunted, and he had no doubt what the outcome would be. That it would be brought about with the toylike .22 he now carried was all the more appropriate.

Gunther felt himself in the hands of fate. When he was taken to the courthouse, when he was questioned by the sheriff and his deputies, he had been sure fate had turned against him. But, incredibly, the focus had remained on whether or not he was Leroy White, and once it was clear that (despite what had been done with his rented car) he was not, that was the end of it. Now he was on his own, in charge of his own destiny—and he would make the most of it.

At the trestle he crossed the river and went up the bank to the oasis, passing through the restaurant to the opposite side of the interstate; from the back of the parking lot he could see in the distance the Wyler truckstop. It was where he had stayed when he first reconnoitered the area. For a time, he had meant to approach the Krueger farm in the way he had just come, starting from the truckstop, walking to the oasis, getting to the river, and then over the trestle to the farm. Until it occurred to him that he could

178

park on that side of the oasis, change, go to the farm and perform his task, dump everything in the river on his return, and be on his way.

It increased his sense of being fated that now the truckstop should provide a needed haven.

The first time he had been driving a rented truck, was dressed like a trucker, and caused no comment when he rented the sleeping room. But this time the clerk looked at him curiously.

"I'm on my way to pick up a rig."

The clerk showed a gap-toothed grin. "Don't want anyone thinking this is Howard Johnson's."

He slept the sleep of the fated, and in the morning (after a trucker's breakfast—a four-by-four: four eggs, four slices of bacon) he called the Wyler Historical Society and told Earl Sanders he had been advised by Bernice Beresford to call him about the Krueger archives.

"I'm afraid they're not going to be available today." The man sounded as if he were going to cry.

"Is something wrong?"

"Of course something's wrong! I've been robbed, if you can believe it. The Krueger papers and God knows what else are gone. I'm about to run a check."

Gunther hung up. Leroy. It had to be. How, he didn't know, but he was certain that pest Leroy was at the bottom of this.

His own visits to Bernice and interest in the WHA constituted an insurance policy. He wanted to make sure that there was no chance Krueger had written down his secret elsewhere than in the ledger. Not that he thought this possible, but it is a wise man that looks under every rock. What if there was something in the stolen archives that would give Leroy a clue to the real motive of the killing he had somehow observed?

"Okay, asshole," he growled aloud, causing a passing trucker to glare at Gunther. He continued the thought silently.

You're going to go, Leroy, and the sooner the better.

TWENTY-SIX

It had been dumb getting ahead of Gunther boarding the bus, Leroy told himself later. What if the sonofabitch hadn't made it aboard, or had changed his mind? There Leroy would have been going off down the street in a bus—and given what Gunther did next, it was doubtful that he would have picked up the trail again.

He had been right to guess that Gunther would return to his hotel after the sheriff saw that Gunther wasn't really Leroy. What came as a surprise was Gunther's showing up almost immediately outside again, peeking around the corner. What the hell? But when a bus approached, it became clear what he was up to. Gunther knew he was being pursued, and he meant to shake free of his pursuer. He came across the street like a kamikaze pilot, darting out of the way of cars, honked at but determined. Watching him come, Leroy made the mistake of getting up off the bench too soon. Then he crowded ahead of Gunther, since to do an Alphonse and Gaston routine would have drawn attention to himself.

It had been a lesson watching Gunther at the shopping center. When the punkster grabbed the ten-speed before Gunther could, Leroy could have cheered. There was no other unlocked bike in that rack, and even if there were, Leroy on a bicycle that put his rear end above his head would have been no match for Gunther. Gunther, he somehow knew, would be expert on a ten-speed.

The purchase of the .22 reminded Leroy that this was a deadly game. Maybe he should have killed Gunther when he found him, choked the life out of him, and been done with it. Once Gunther was dead, Leroy would be free to join Marilys.

He stole a car to follow the Sunset Village bus, wanting to keep it in sight in case Gunther did not go all the way to the village. It was a slow drive, and gave him a chance to ponder what he had been doing. Was he playing games with Gunther to put off the pact he had made with himself? Two days before, the idea of, once Gunther was dead, killing himself and joining Marilys had been overwhelmingly attractive. But already he was becoming used to the fact the Marilys was dead. He found it difficult to conjure up a vivid image of her. And he tried, perhaps too hard. He didn't talk to her much either, so she wasn't in on his plans the way she ought to be. In any case, he wanted to do what he meant to do before his memory of her became too faded. And, he decided, he did want to die. Even if the memory of Marilys faded entirely away, he had to face the fact that his life was a pointless mess and must be ended.

He had abandoned the car and was following Gunther at a distance as he wandered through Sunset Village, but when his quarry took the three-wheeled bike and pedaled out of the village, Leroy retrieved the car. There was something comic, at first, in the sight of Gunther pedaling along the side of the highway in that ridiculous three-wheeler, a pennant waving on the top of a flexible car-radio-aerial sort of thing. Leroy did not laugh. There, he told himself—and he got Marilys in on it too—there goes a determined sonofabitch. The thought that he was after Leroy was a sobering one. Gunther was not to be easily stopped. Leroy wondered what he had been thinking of, trying to play games with this guy and win. He decided to end the whole thing right now.

He had been holding back, himself the object of as many irate horns as Gunther, but there was a bridge coming up and Gunther was going to have to wheel that contraption onto the road to get over the river. Leroy positioned himself and calculated the distance. He had just tromped on the gas, ready to nail Gunther when he tried to turn onto the road, when the bastard headed into the ditch. Leroy had to continue on over the bridge, something he did at a high rate of speed, tailgating the car ahead of him. The first chance he had on the other side, he turned off the road, left the car and went scrambling back toward the river, slipping and sliding down the embankment.

183

When he got to the water's edge, he could see the three-wheeler under the bridge, abandoned. And then he caught sight of Gunther, moving like the Deerslayer up the opposite bank. Leroy relaxed. He knew enough about Gunther now to make tailing him easier, and he was pretty sure where Gunther was headed. Leroy turned and went up to the abandoned car.

At the oasis he parked and went into the coffee shop to get something to eat. Anyone passing through the restaurant that spanned the four lanes of the interstate would be visible from where Leroy sat. He had finished a burger and was enjoying his chocolate sundae when Gunther went by. Leroy picked up his ice cream and followed. Gunther went through people like a bowling ball: if they didn't get out of his way, too bad. One lady shepherding three knee-high kids nearly went over when Gunther clipped her elbow and sent her spinning.

"Hey," she shouted. Heads turned, but people weren't sure what they were supposed to be looking at.

Gunther kept right on going through the parking lot, paused at its end and then went over the fence and disappeared.

Leroy, being careful, sauntered over to where Gunther had paused and looked out over the wooded valley. On the horizon, actually only a mile or so away, a sign rose high above the trees. TRUCK STOP 77. Where he and Marilys had filled up the van a couple of times when they were just prowling the area, the gas at the truck stop a lot cheaper than on the interstate. Leroy decided the truck stop was Gunther's destination. There was nothing else between the oasis and the truck stop. He smiled. Let Gunther do the walking. He would drive. He got the last of the chocolate sauce out of the plastic container, put it into a trash receptacle like a good citizen, and strolled through the oasis to the other side.

He stopped inside the door. A cruiser was parked next to the car he had been driving and coming toward him was the deputy he had given a hard time before. Heart in his throat, Leroy turned and ran to the men's room, where he locked himself into a stall and stared disgustedly at the graffiti. Good God, there are a lot of sick people running around loose. He had to think. That cop was coming in because he assumed the driver of the stolen car was in the oasis. Could Leroy have been connected with the car? There was no way he could know. But if the deputy hadn't come into the oasis looking for someone in particular, he was wasting his time. But then he was wasting his time parking the cruiser next to the stolen car if he was interested in nailing the one who took it. This deputy was so dumb it was hard to tell what he might or might not do.

Someone entered the next stall, making metallic noises as he did so. The trousers beneath the intervening wall had a stripe down the side. When they hit the floor, Leroy got out of the booth and out of the oasis. He was across the trestle before the deputy could be washing his hands.

Now he was in the same box as Gunther, only he had less choice. The cops were after Leroy; Gunther so far had to fear only Leroy. It didn't seem fair. Gunther had killed two people Leroy knew about,

185

yet as far as Wyler was concerned, he could walk its streets undisturbed. Maybe that was the way to do it, act as if he ran no risk, act as if he hadn't done things that had made him a fugitive.

Leroy trudged to the bus stop and rode downtown, where he reoccupied his bench across from the Hoosier. It was a warm, sultry night, and in the predawn hours Leroy took a walk through the neighborhoood in which Andrew Broom lived. Just curious. It reminded him that he was going to have to get an M1 from Glen Olson. Now that Gunther was armed, he had to get ready if he was going to keep to his original plan—kill Gunther the way Gunther had killed the Palmer guy.

The unknown factor was when Gunther would move into the Krueger house.

It was just by luck that he recognized Gunther the next day, rolling by with a cowboy gait, skintight blue denim pants, blue shirt unbuttoned to his navel, opaque sunglasses, and the International Harvester cap pulled low over his eyes. Maybe he would never have known who it was if he had not followed Gunther yesterday and seen his versatility. Leroy followed Gunther into the newspaper building. He stood across the lobby, buttoning his shirt. The cap was off, the glasses in his pocket; he was talking with the girl at the information desk.

After he had gotten into an elevator, Leroy hurried up to the desk. The girl lifted languorous eyes as if she lived in the hope that a movie-maker would some day approach her counter.

"Where did he go?"

"Who?"

"My friend. The big guy in the blue shirt, he was just here . . ."

"The archives."

"Is that on two?"

She made a face and pointed down with a finger whose nail looked like a lethal weapon. "Basement," she said, her cheeks puffing nicely as she made the *b* explosive, lips kissing one another over the *m*, a grin with the final dental *t*.

"You should be in the movies."

"I know."

It was later, talking with Bernice, that he heard of the WHA and its warehousing arrangement with the city. The amorous archivist could call up the WHA database on her modem. She typed Krueger without being asked, as if she had forgotten Gunther was gone and good old Leroy had taken his place.

"In the warehouse," she observed.

He could have spent the night with Bernice, he might have, but he wanted to check out the warehouse.

"Give me a rain check."

"Sure. For the next time I sleep outside."

TWENTY-SEVEN

After Andrew Broom left, Martha remained at her kitchen table. She hadn't quite been robbed, but it was too much like it to suit her. Imagine someone breaking into the WHA archives and stealing things!

She shook her head. She had to stop trying to fool herself. The only thing stolen had been Emil's correspondence with old Krueger and other papers involving him. Sometimes Martha thought of the Krueger farm as the flaw in their lives. Whenever it became a factor, things went wrong. And they would go wrong again now that she was on the verge of selling it. Something was afoot that she did not understand and it frightened her. Remembering those calls from Franklin Meecham pointed to the beginning of the trouble.

Say it. There had been a connection between fail-

ure to put the offer to Willard Palmer and his murder. In her way, she was responsible for that. Martha
laid an index finger sideways in her mouth and bit
on it.

It wasn't just the past event that bothered her. The
man who had killed Willard Palmer was again in
town. That he was the one who robbed the WHA
seemed to follow by some kind of necessity she could
not have explained.

When the phone rang, she sat immobile, not wanting to answer, wishing it would stop. But the only
way she could stop the ringing was to answer.

"Mrs. Doremus? This is Gunther Kunz."

"Who?"

"Gunther Kunz. I hope you haven't forgotten my
interest in the Krueger place?"

The voice was the voice of Franklin Meecham, no
matter what name he gave her now. There was no
possible doubt on the matter. Martha, her hand
trembling, hung up the phone. She hugged herself to
stop the shivering, but it did not help.

How stupid she was. She might just as well have
announced to him that she recognized his voice. No
wonder she had been unable to locate a lawyer named
Franklin Meecham in Baltimore. There was no such
person. There was only Gunther Kunz.

And that meant he must have been the one who
shot Willard Palmer!

The phone began to ring again. Martha got a grip
on herself and picked it up.

"Mr. Kunz? We must have been cut off."

"Then you do remember me?"

"I flatter myself that I have never forgotten a client."

"Could I come see you this morning."

"This morning?" She hummed the words meditatively. "Oh, I am so sorry, this morning is terrible."

"Tell me when I should come."

Martha was behaving beyond her own most unrealistic expectations. At his last remark she smiled grimly.

"How does two o'clock sound?"

"At your place."

"No. At Andrew Broom's office. I'll give you the address."

After she had done so, she said she would see him at two and hung up. She stared at the phone. She had been speaking with a murderer. She had had a murderer in her house. He must be lured to Andrew Broom's office and confronted with his deed. Andrew would know how to go about it.

Meanwhile, she called Andrew's office, but the line was busy. Next she called the WHA, hoping to get more information from Earl Sanders, but the boy Louis said Mr. Sanders was at the warehouse with Mr. Broom.

"Do you have the number of the warehouse."

"It is impossible to reach Mr. Sanders by phone when he is at the warehouse."

"Thank you, Louis."

"Would you like to leave a message for Mr. Sanders?"

She decided against that. For half an hour she felt frozen in inaction. And then she knew what she would do. She would drive to the warehouse and meet the two men there. From Earl she could get whatever details there were on the theft, and then with Andrew she would reveal what she now knew of the prospective purchaser of the Krueger farm. Her heart sank at the thought. The possibility of selling the farm was gone. It was likely to remain hers for a long time to come.

She put on the light wrapper that served her as a coat during these warm early autumn days. A hat. Of course. A navy blue straw with an exciting band that complemented her coat. How Emil would have objected. A straw after Labor Day!

Martha backed out of the door in order to pull it tightly shut.

"Ah, Mrs. Doremus."

A frigid current traveled up her back and she turned to face the smiling Gunther Kunz. He was dressed as a cowboy. "It's not two," she cried. "It's not time."

He studied her carefully as she bleated these words, his smile steady. After a moment, he nodded slowly.

"I see. Let's go inside, Mrs. Doremus."

"I have to run an errand."

His hand closed on her arm and she was moved decisively back inside. He pulled the door closed after them. She wanted to scream, but she knew that if she tried no sound would emerge from her mouth.

"You were very good on the phone," he said, looking around. Then he saw it. He pulled the wires free, disabling the phone. "You didn't know until this morning, did you? It was a mistake to speak to you on the phone."

"What are you talking about?"

He ignored her. "The question is, what do we do now?"

"We are going to meet, at two. You want to buy the farm."

"Palmer should have listened to reason. I meant it when I said I would make an irresistible offer. An offer he couldn't resist. Did you recognize the phrase?"

She shook her head vigorously. She was still wearing her hat. It seemed important to keep it on. She was on her way out. He sat her forcibly down in a chair.

"*The Godfather.* One must keep up with the popular culture. Perhaps Palmer didn't."

"I never told him. I knew he wouldn't want to sell."

"You never told him?" He stared at her icily.

"He would have refused."

His hand moved so swiftly she did not even try to get out of its way; then, incredibly, it struck her, snapping her head to one side. Her hat stayed on, but next he wrenched it from her head. He crouched before her chair and forced her to look into his eyes. Dante's hell ends in ice at its lowest depth. Martha felt she was looking into hell.

"He might be alive if you had told him."

It was what she had thought herself. The shock of being struck was giving way to pain. She felt that her cheekbone was broken. This powerful man could break her into pieces. Is that what he intended?

He stood and looked down at her. "Would you like ice for your face?"

"How can you strike me and then pretend concern?"

"Whether I am nice or cruel doesn't matter." He crouched again, sitting on his heels. "Where did your husband get into contact with Krueger?"

"I don't know."

He struck her again, on the other cheek, his cruelty a perversion of the Gospel.

"You were your husband's partner from the beginning. You told me that. Where did Krueger go when he left here?"

"I don't know." She cringed, wanting to gather herself into the body's original position, beyond the veil of material flesh.

"There must be some record here."

"I gave everything to the historical society."

He laughed scornfully, and then his eyes assumed their infernal cold. "Was that a ruse? Telling me the records have been stolen?"

She didn't know what to say. She kept her eyes on his hands. She could not bear to be struck again. Both sides of her face were pulsing with pain. He took her wrist and pulled her to her feet.

"Where are your files?"

"There's nothing there."

"Why is there nothing there? Why does everyone want to erase the name of Krueger from this town? Why are you lying to me?" His voice rose a level with each question, reminding her of the old Holy Saturday liturgy. *Flectamus genua. Levate.* He was propelling her through the house to the office. He tugged at a file drawer, but it was locked.

"The key is in the desk. Look for yourself. You'll find nothing."

"Why!" he roared. He pulled open the desk drawer and began rummaging around. Oh, everything would be a mess, she knew it. "You all hated the Kruegers, didn't you?"

"Yes!" she screamed, not knowing why she did. She knew she was through humoring him. He had hit her in the face twice and had pushed her around her house like an animal. What more could he do if she opposed him?

"You did," he said, calmly, nodding, happy with her answer. "I knew it."

"Are you one of them? Are you a Krueger?"

"I am one of them, all right, but I'm not a Krueger. Is this the key?"

"You're wasting my time and yours."

"I, at least, have plenty of time."

After unlocking the file, he began to pull folders out, glance at them, throw them to the floor.

"Stop that! You're making a mess for no reason."

He seemed to agree with her. He turned and once more crouched in front of the chair she sat in. There was a solicitous expression on his face.

"Are you a religious woman?"

She said nothing.

"Do you believe in God?"

She nodded. Not to nod would have been a kind of apostasy.

"Good."

He stood and went into the living room where he had put down the plastic bag he was carrying. Martha was at the door leading from the office to the street when he came back. He shook his head, looking disappointed with her.

"You're not going anyplace, Mrs. Doremus. Correction. You are about to take a very long journey."

The little rifle jumped and bucked as he pulled the trigger and Martha fell to the floor, her body stinging as from a dozen bees. She fell through pools of color and into darkness and then saw far ahead the brightest light she had ever seen.

TWENTY-EIGHT

Earl Sanders was, by his own account, beside himself —and where that put Andrew he did not know. All he knew was that he wished he were elsewhere. Earl was a pain in the *derrière* at the best of times, but cast in the role of outraged victim of cosmic absurdity, the pain was unbearable and its locus beyond circumlocution.

"Have you ever been circumlocuted, Earl?"

Earl was astounded, which was good, since it shut him up for a minute. "At the hospital," he said, after gasping like the asthmatic he wasn't. "Not in a religious ceremony."

"You're not listening. I intend to follow your example. Goodbye."

"But what are we going to do?"

"Hope the stolen property is recovered."

196

"But what if it isn't?"

"That's a problem people all over the world confront every day."

"Are you really leaving?"

He explained that there was nothing to be gained from one or both of them hanging around a warehouse that had been robbed the previous day. Earl calmed down a bit, and Andrew steered the archivist toward his vintage MG. Andrew himself slipped into the Oldsmobile he was driving while the BMW was given a thorough check after its unscheduled trip. He picked up the cellular phone.

"Don't use that."

Andrew's eyes lifted to the rearview mirror. The fat bald man. Leroy.

"Or I'll use this. Slowly," he added as Andrew turned to look at the rifle the man held.

"What do you want?"

"Just drive for now."

The engine turned over and purred. Andrew eased away from the curb just as Earl's little MG came flying into the street, horn beeping. Earl had both hands on the wheel and a checkered cap on his head, eyes on the road. Even if Earl's peripheral vision had been phenomenal, it wouldn't have mattered. The man had dropped out of sight at the sound of Earl's horn.

"Why did you come back?"

"I appreciated the use of your car. I never drove a car like that before."

"Who was the girl?"

Silence in the backseat. "She was a woman."

"Did you kill her?"

"Did I kill her?" A bark of a laugh. "No, I didn't kill her."

"The police think you did."

"They're crazy."

"Tell me about it."

"Why should I?"

"Because I'm a lawyer." It was difficult to drive and carry on a conversation either over his shoulder or via the rearview mirror.

"Whose?"

"I have many clients."

"Like Gunther."

"You know him?"

"Know him? Him I'll kill. I've never killed a soul, but I am going to kill that bastard."

Andrew knew from the practice of law how the world can change as one moves from viewpoint to viewpoint. He was trying to figure out the one he was being given now.

"Do you want to know what it looks like to the police, Leroy?"

"How do you know my name?"

"I make it a point to learn the names of people who steal my car. Listen to me now, all right? First, a deputy finds marijuana in your van, your girl lets the air out of his tires, and you flee. Second, you steal my car, money, and credit cards, and head for Indianapolis where you live in a nonluxury motel and she goes to work. Third, she is killed, you shave your beard, and leave town in a stolen car. Murder,

car and various other thefts, possession of marijuana, etcetera, etcetera. That is how it looks to the
police."

"Let me come up front."

Andrew pulled over and Leroy, carrying the rifle,
opened the back door. He was clumsy and it took an
effort for him to get out. For a moment he was out of
the car and Andrew could have taken off, risking a
lucky shot from the rifle. But he waited for Leroy to
get in beside him.

"I did not kill Marilys." He looked at Andrew with
pleading eyes. "All the rest, yes, I did it. But not
that. Gunther killed her. It all goes back to his killing the guy on the farm."

"Willard Palmer. How do you know that?"

"Do you smoke?"

Andrew pulled away from the curb. "We'll get you
some cigarettes."

"I didn't think you'd go for grass."

Ten minutes later they were sitting in the plastic
anonymity of McDonald's and Andrew was listening
to Leroy's account of how he knew Gunther killed
Palmer. Andrew's incredulity lifted when Leroy described Gunther returning across the trestle and
throwing the duffel bag into the water.

"I found it," Andrew said.

"That's because Marilys threw it in again."

"Where did you get that rifle?"

"I borrowed it from a man named Olson."

"Glen Olson?"

"Yeah. One of your clients. He doesn't realize I

199

have it. But I read of his arsenal in the local paper. I wanted a rifle like the one he used."

"What for?"

"For Gunther."

"Don't."

"Let the law do it?" Leroy wore a disgusted look.

Andrew shrugged. "What else?"

"Vengeance is mine, saith the Lord."

Leroy's eyes wore the expression you sometimes see at wakes and funerals, the expression of a mourner who has lost his reason for living. Such a person cannot imagine returning to the routine of daily life and finding much point in it.

"Maybe I'm his instrument."

"Maybe the law is."

"It's a pretty sorry one."

"But you're better."

"At least I'll know it's been done."

"If I were going to kill someone, I'd keep planning to a minimum. And once I decided to do it, I'd do it. You're playing games. I don't think you really mean to kill Gunther."

Leroy looked into the colorful cup that held his coffee. He certainly looked like the wrath of God. Was he growing a beard again or just forgetting to shave? His eyes were red, his clothes looked as if he had slept in them.

"Where have you been staying?"

"Here and there."

"You were walking around my neighborhood the other night, weren't you?"

"What were you doing up at three in the morning?"

"I realized I had seen you before. Sitting on a bench in the courthouse, for example. It was a mistake pulling that stunt with Gunther's rented car, Leroy."

"Is this legal advice?"

"Just an observation."

"Because you're Gunther's lawyer."

"I am representing him in a real-estate transaction, that's all."

"He wants to buy that farm?"

"Yes."

"Why does he want it so badly?"

Badly enough to kill for it, that was the implication. It was a good question, even without the assumption that Gunther had killed Palmer. The desire was accompanied by a keen interest in the past history of the place, the remoter the better. It was the Krueger family that interested Gunther, nothing in recent years. Why? He did not intend to speculate about it with Leroy. When he left Earl, Andrew had intended to go immediately to Martha's, to see if there was anything in the way of a memory or a record that might explain this interest in the Kruegers.

"By pulling that stunt on Gunther, you made it clear you were in town."

"I wanted him to know."

"No surprises. Will you call him out in the middle of Tarkington, a western duel?"

"I'll give him as much of a chance as he gave Marilys and Palmer."

Andrew looked at his watch. "Why don't we visit

201

the lady who is handling the property. She knows this town as well as anyone."

"Why should I come along?"

"Do you have something better to do?"

Leroy's eyes drifted over the plastic decor, over the functional tables and swing-out seats molded to fit the average ass, out the window, aimlessly.

"Why not?"

The rifle was on the back floor of the Oldsmobile at Andrew's urging. "I don't have a rifle rack." Leroy got into the passenger seat and seemed to have forgotten the weapon. It was always wise to be wary of a man with a weapon, but Andrew had stopped fearing Leroy even before he got into the front seat.

"I like this town," Leroy said as they drove to Martha's.

"What sort of work do you do?"

"Before I chucked it all, I was in business for myself."

The Dairy Queen, Andrew remembered. "Wyler is a good place for an entrepreneur."

"Tell it to the sheriff."

"Think about it."

"In my cell?" But Leroy did not sound like a man who feared going to prison.

Andrew sensed something wrong as soon as he drove up in front of the house. For one thing, the screen door was ajar at the main entrance. He jumped out of the car and went on the run to the front door. He went inside without ceremony. The living quarters were neat as a pin, but as he started toward the office, Andrew saw the disconnected telephone. The open file cabinets, the paper on the floor ... and then Martha.

She lay as if she had dropped to her knees and then tumbled backward, her hands raised in the praying position, on her face the stunned, frozen look of a little girl of seventy-five.

Andrew did not enter the office, but went around Leroy and picked up the wire of the phone. He shoved it into the back of the instrument and dialed his office.

On the second ring, he heard the car start. He turned to look through the frilly curtains at Leroy driving off in the Oldsmobile.

TWENTY-NINE

Leroy turned the corner at gathering speed and the rifle clattered across the floor behind him. The reminder was reassuring.

Too bad about the old lady, but he hadn't known her. He hadn't known Palmer either. You can't mourn for strangers. Marilys he had known. He had left everything for her, wife and family, home and business. It had been like a religious call, if that wasn't blasphemy.

He didn't really believe it was God's will, what he had been doing with Marilys in the van. Living with Marilys was losing all your illusions about yourself. I am a weak sonofabitch, Lord, Leroy more or less prayed. I did it for the fun of it and it was fun, but it was more than that. It was wrong, but there was a rightness too. Lying in the dark, smoke rising lazily, he had tried to explain it to Marilys.

"Why do you need reasons?" she asked.

"Think of what you said."

"I am."

"You asked for a reason why you should ask for reasons. We can't help it."

"I can."

Living with Marilys was a recognition of how worthless all his efforts were. He had married a wife, raised a family, run a business. So what? All along he thought he was gaining credit, the way they gave you stick-on stars at the library for reading during vacation when you were a kid. He hadn't remembered that until he told Marilys about it.

Once out of Martha Doremus's neighborhood, Leroy slowed down. He knew where he was going; the only question was the best route. This whole thing came down to that farm. Gunther wanted it so much he would do anything for it. There had to be something there, something he couldn't just go in and take. Leroy decided to stick to Plan One. Broom might call it playing games, but there was justice to it and Leroy did not doubt he was doing something just.

He put the Oldsmobile where they had parked the van, maybe a space or two over. He got out, leaving it unlocked, loosened the strap, and slung the rifle over his shoulder. He had taken the one clip that lay beside the M1. That should be enough.

Crossing the trestle, he felt as Gunther must have when he set out to murder Palmer. The water looked less muddy today, more movement to the current. On the other side Leroy went slowly up the bank to the field and then, bending over so his weight would pull him forward, he climbed the hill. Just short of the top, he lay down, out of weariness rather than caution, and dragged himself forward until the house came into view.

Gunther was in the backyard, a shovel in his hand, pacing the distance from an outdoor barbecue to a big tree. But he stopped before he reached it. He looked back and forth, as if reviewing what he had done, inhaled, and began to dig.

Dig! There was something buried. That's what he wanted. Leroy, a little smile on his face, got settled in. He brought the rifle around into position and then lay there, enjoying the sight of Gunther working his ass off. Let him dig himself silly, then he would get his. The digging seemed to Leroy pretty much what everyone is doing, busy, busy, busy, intent on getting something or other, but what does it matter if they do or not? Sooner or later they are interrupted by the Grim Reaper, as Gunther was going to be interrupted when Leroy undid the safety, got a bead on him, and did to him what he had been doing to others.

Gunther was working frantically. He wouldn't know how soon the old lady's body would be found and he wanted to get what he was digging for as quickly as he could. What was he after? A fragment of a phrase drifted like a thin cloud across Leroy's memory. Where rust and moth consume and thief breaks in to steal. Jesus speaking of treasure.

206

Gunther had the hole maybe two feet across and as deep. He was standing in it now and it occurred to Leroy he was digging his own grave. Marilys had wanted him to leave Wyler when he realized what Gunther had done. What would have happened if he had listened to her? She would be alive and they would still be in the van, going nowhere, their lives as pointless as Gunther's digging.

The image of Marilys was sharp and definite in his mind now, and his chest ached at the memory of her. His eyes were blurring with tears when he flipped the safety off and sighted in on Gunther.

The first shot drove a hole through the shovel as Gunther was lifting it from the ground. It spun from his hands. The second shot took out an upstairs window, and the third must have gone over the house. The rifle kept jerking upward in a way Leroy had not been prepared for. By the time he got it down again, and wiped his eyes, Gunther was nowhere to be seen.

Leroy blinked his eyes dry. His right shoulder hurt from the kick of the butt into it. Now that he had actually fired the rifle, Leroy remembered how difficult it was to aim the thing, particularly at this range.

The crack of a shot from the house made Leroy burrow into the dirt, and then he began to slide backward. He stopped himself with the thought that he had nowhere to go. This was his last job and he had better do it. He inched up the hill again, coming over it at a different spot than he had left it. He got a glimpse of Gunther in an upstairs window and had time to slide down again before the crack of Gunther's second shot.

It helped that he was going nowhere else, but even apart from that it seemed to Leroy his position was not so bad. He commanded the backyard from this hill. Gunther had to get into the backyard to finish digging. As far as Leroy could see, he had the sonofabitch. No one who had already killed three people for it was going to give up on whatever was in the ground.

Leroy pushed a couple of good-sized stones to the crest of the hill, affording himself some protection from the house, and settled down, lying rolled to one side, his eye on the backyard. He was exhausted from lack of sleep and could easily have dozed off, but he fought it. Once he was finished here, he would have all the sleep he wanted.

If he was lucky. Close to it now, Leroy wondered what he would find on the other side. Marilys? Rest? No one had put him in charge of arrangements. Maybe he wouldn't like it all. If Jesus meant what he'd said, Leroy was going to be sorry. So he lay there, talking with Marilys, bargaining with Jesus, saying he was sorry about the wife and kids. He was sorry he wasn't sorry, anyhow.

No more shots came from the house and Gunther hadn't dared go back into the yard. After fifteen minutes Leroy became uneasy. He scrunched down behind his little wall of stones and stared carefully at the house, his rifle at the ready.

There was a clicking sound behind him.

Leroy rolled on his back, bringing his rifle around. Gunther stood there, a giant against the sky, a malevolent silhouette, holding a small rifle. A frozen second during which neither man fired.

"Gunther!"

A voice from below, from the house, it sounded like the lawyer Broom. Gunther spun toward the house and Leroy could see his features, the twisted look of angry frustration. Leroy moved the M1. He did not fire. It was as if Marilys were saying something in his ear. While he was trying to hear, Gunther turned and fired four rounds. The first ripped through Leroy's head, the second got him in the throat, the others in the chest.

He was dead before he could have heard the shot from the direction of the house.

THIRTY

The rusty metal box lay on a table in Andrew Broom's office; under it was the tarp in which it had been wrapped after being lifted from the ground behind the Krueger house. The box was without a lock, which, when you thought about it, was an unnecessary precaution if it was going to be buried.

And buried was the word. The sheriff's men had gone down six feet to find the thing. The sheriff and Hanson had come for the opening, and, of course, Susannah and Gerald were also there. Earl Sanders's claim to an ex officio right to be present was absurd, but he (along with Bernice Beresford) was in attendance. Andrew lifted the lid and eased it back gently because the hinge pins were rusted through. The certificates were wrapped in oilcloth, the kind once familiar on kitchen tables across the nation.

A groan went around the room when Andrew picked up a Krupp certificate and identified it.

"Any Confederate money?" Bernice asked, making a stab at Earl's ribs with her elbow, but the archivist danced out of danger.

"Krupp and IG Farben," Andrew announced after looking through the bundle. The certificates had a damp cold feel to them. Andrew stepped back so the others could examine the treasure and beckoned Gerald.

"Give Valerie at the bank a call and ask her if these things have value."

Meanwhile, at the table, the faded but still colorful certificates were being handled and examined amid jokes and mocking laughter. Bernice wanted one as a souvenir.

"Of what?" Earl demanded, disgusted.

"Come over sometime and I'll show you. Did you ever hear of Big Bertha."

"I intend to give you a Big Bertha," Earl snapped. "Certainly a wide one."

Bernice grabbed him and hugged him to her bosom. From the other room, a phone in his hand, Gerald was waving at Andrew. Andrew went to him and took the offered phone.

"I want you to hear this for yourself," Gerald said.

Valerie repeated that both companies were still very much in business and were certain to honor shares issued in the past.

"Valerie, let me tell you we have a lot of Krupp here."

"Let me check on it. But don't throw them away

or burn them or do anything foolish. Whose are they, by the way?"

"Good question."

The question was still unanswered when Valerie called back. Andrew read the numbers and dates of the certificates to her. He could hear her entering them on her computer. A half-minute went by.

"If they're worth less than twenty million, I'll buy you a Popsicle."

The guessing began immediately. Since Willard Palmer's agreement to purchase was nullified by his death, title to the house was unequivocally Martha Doremus's. But Martha, God rest her soul, was dead and she had insisted to Andrew that she had no heirs.

"Is the buried box included in the purchase of the house?" Earl Sanders asked. "Maybe it's excluded, like mineral rights."

"Excluded in favor of whom?"

"The Krueger family. I think their intent when burying those certificates is clear from the ledger."

Earl had the advantage there, being the only one able to read German. His interpretation was that the investments had been hidden in haste, to be recovered later by Krueger or his heirs.

"A lawyer could proceed on that," Andrew said. "If there are any Krueger heirs."

"Oh, there must be," Earl said.

"Yeah?" Bernice said. "What becomes of your family if you don't marry."

She was right, families do die out—but Earl was right as well. There would be (in whatever degree of removal) Krueger relatives, and thus possible claimants.

Susannah served coffee, and it was then that Hanson asked Andrew about the big shootout at the Krueger farm.

"I was lucky," Andrew said. "I hadn't fired that rifle in years. Besides, I was aiming at his legs."

The shot from Andrew's .22 had smashed through Gunther's mouth and wrought havoc in his brain. He lived for an hour after arriving at Emergency.

" 'Lucky' as in 'sharpshooter'?"

"That was a long time ago. Anyway, I would have preferred to see him go to trial."

"It's funny Leroy didn't shoot. The sheriff thinks he froze, too scared to fire."

Andrew Broom looked at Hanson, tilted his head, wrinked his nose.

"Maybe."

Andrew preferred to think that at the crucial moment Leroy had decided to leave Gunther to the law—human and divine.

EPILOGUE

A month later Susannah came into Andrew's office, closed the door, and stood with her back pressed against it.

"You have a visitor." She might have been announcing a surprise party.

"Who?"

"A claimant for the Krueger fortune."

"One of the family?"

Susannah did not answer, opened the door, and called. "Won't you come in, Miss Boyd?"

She stepped to one side to let a little old lady enter. White hair, pink cheeks, a hat with a medium-sized brim, and a ribbon that matched her rose-colored dress. She was the spitting image of Martha Doremus.

"This is Miss Vivian Boyd, Andrew. Tell Mr. Broom who you are."

"I think I know," Andrew said, coming around his desk to take Miss Boyd's hands. "How are you related to Martha?"

"I don't know how these things are figured exactly, but her grandfather's cousin married a Thompson from Ohio, a Catholic, who was more or less disowned. Well that cousin was my grandfather and . . ."

Andrew could have hugged her. She provided the illusion that the Krueger farm was finally going to do some good for Martha, at least for this cousin God knows how many times removed, whose recent interest in genealogy had led her to these awful killings in Wyler.

"I am told I will need a lawyer."

"Miss Boyd, it is unethical in the extreme, but let me offer my services."

She smiled at Andrew and Susannah, but then a little frown formed.

"What are your fees?" the prospective heiress asked.

RALPH MCINERNY, author of the Father
Dowling mysteries and thirteen other novels
including *Connolly's Life, The Noonday
Devil,* and *Leave of Absence,* is Michael
P. Grace Professor of Medieval Studies
at the University of Notre Dame. *Savings
and Loam* is the third book in his
Andrew Broom mystery series.